SOUTH COUNT

SPACE PIRATE
Sardine in outer space

D1057011

SQUARE
FISH

An Imprint of Macmillan

For information, address Square Fish, 175 Fifth Avenue, New York, N.Y. 10010.

Originally published in France in 2000 under the titles *Sardine de l'espace: Le doigt dans l'oeil* and *Sardine de l'espace: Le bar des ennemis* by Bayard Éditions Jeunesse, Paris.

Cataloging-in-Publication Data is on file at the Library of Congress.

ISBN-13: 978-0-312-38056-4 / ISBN-10: 0-312-38056-9

Originally published in the United States by
First Second, an imprint of Roaring Brook Press

Square Fish logo designed by Filomena Tuosto

First Square Fish Edition: August 2008
10 9 8 7 6 5 4 3 2 1
www.squarefishbooks.com

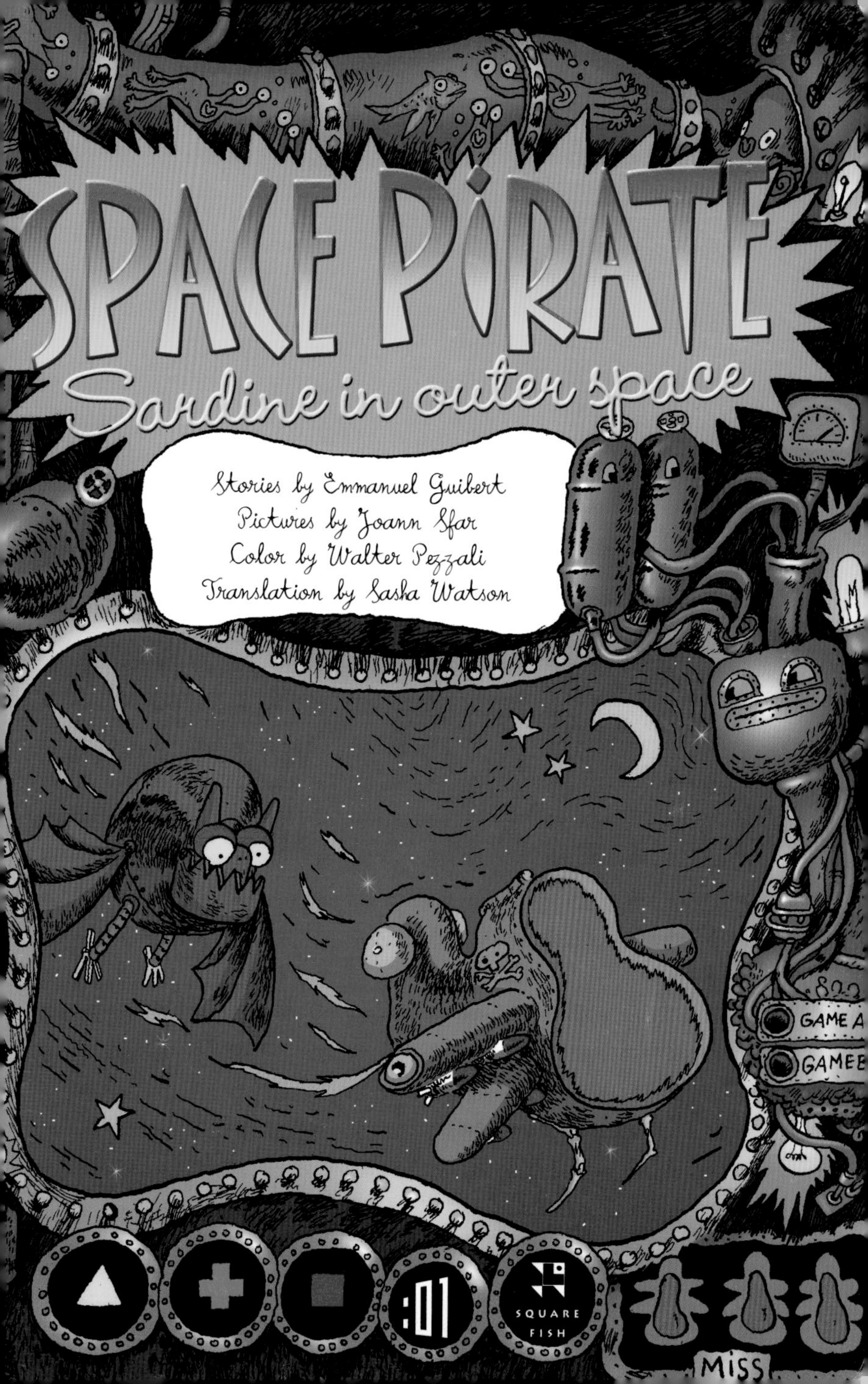
SPACE PIRATE
Sardine in outer space
Stories by Emmanuel Guibert
Pictures by Joann Sfar
Color by Walter Pezzali
Translation by Sasha Watson
GAME A
GAMEB
:01
SQUARE FISH
MISS

Contents

Sardine in Space.. 3

Total Eclipse... 13

Planet Discoball... 23

Eating with the Enemy.................... 33

The New Look.. 43

Stratus, Portus, Aramus.................. 53

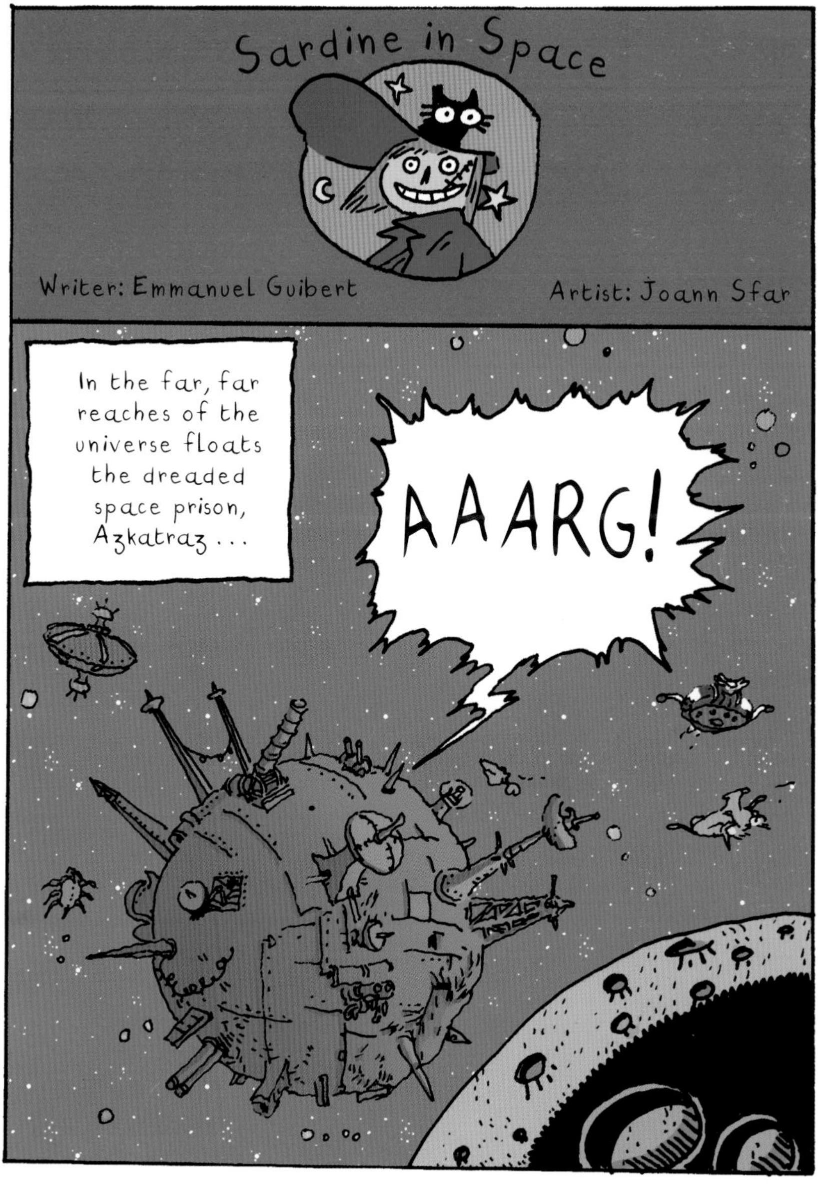
Sardine in Space
Writer: Emmanuel Guibert
Artist: Joann Sfar
In the far, far reaches of the universe floats the dreaded space prison, Azkatraz . . .
AAARG!

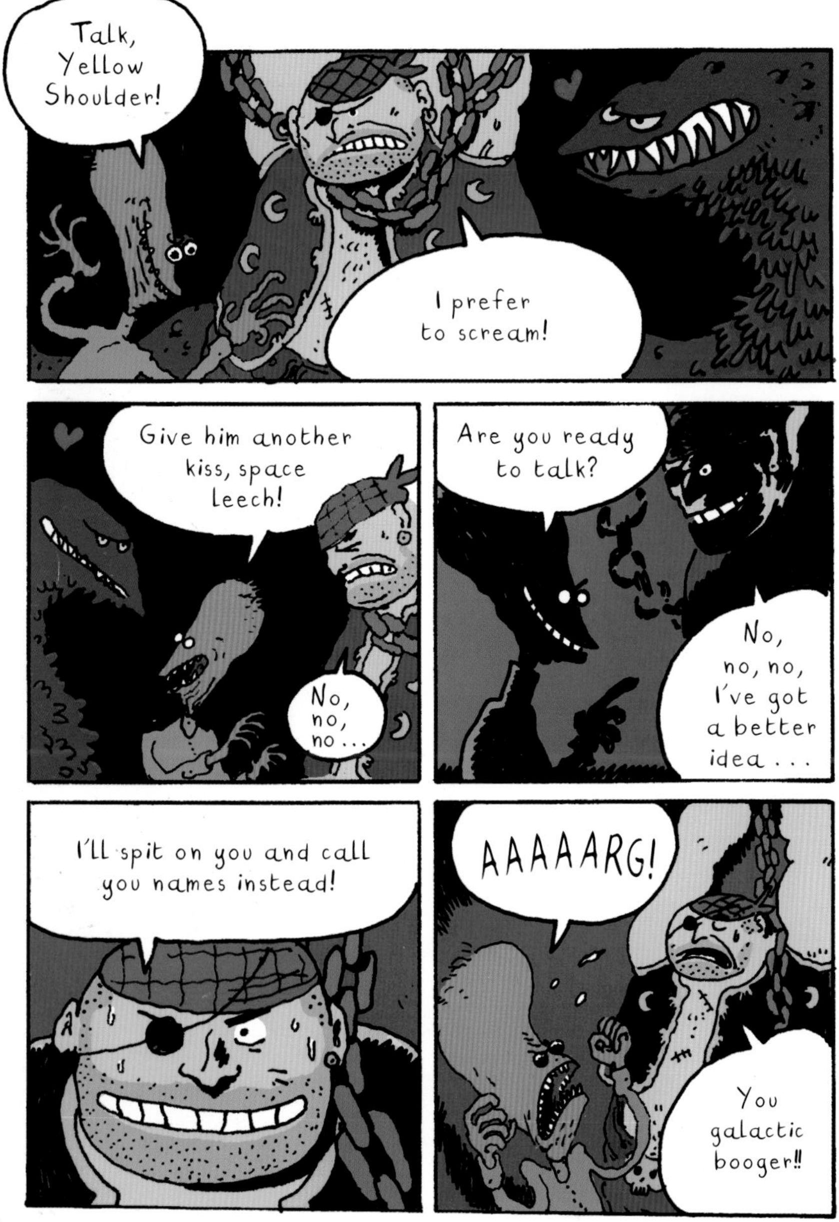

Talk, Yellow Shoulder!
I prefer to scream!
Give him another kiss, space leech!
No, no, no...
Are you ready to talk?
No, no, no, I've got a better idea...
I'll spit on you and call you names instead!
AAAAARG!
You galactic booger!!

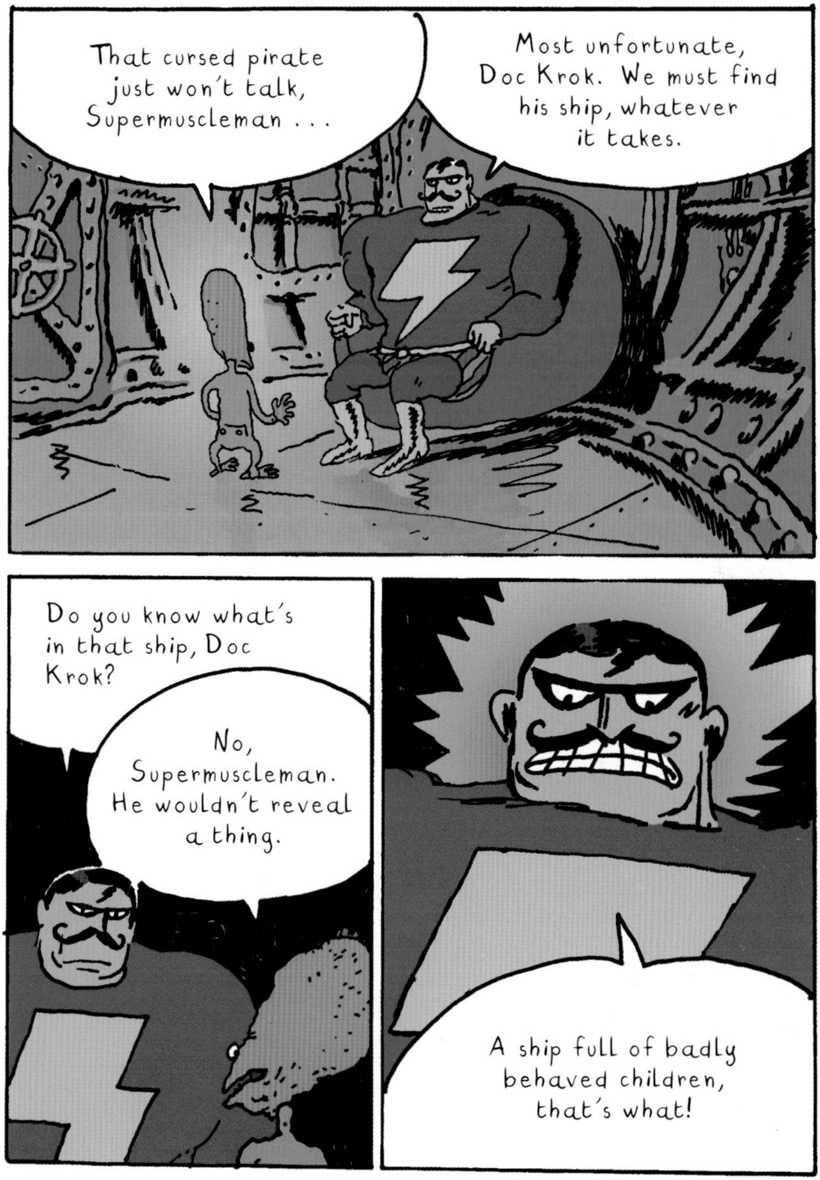
That cursed pirate just won't talk, Supermuscleman . . .
Most unfortunate, Doc Krok. We must find his ship, whatever it takes.
Do you know what's in that ship, Doc Krok?
No, Supermuscleman. He wouldn't reveal a thing.
A ship full of badly behaved children, that's what!

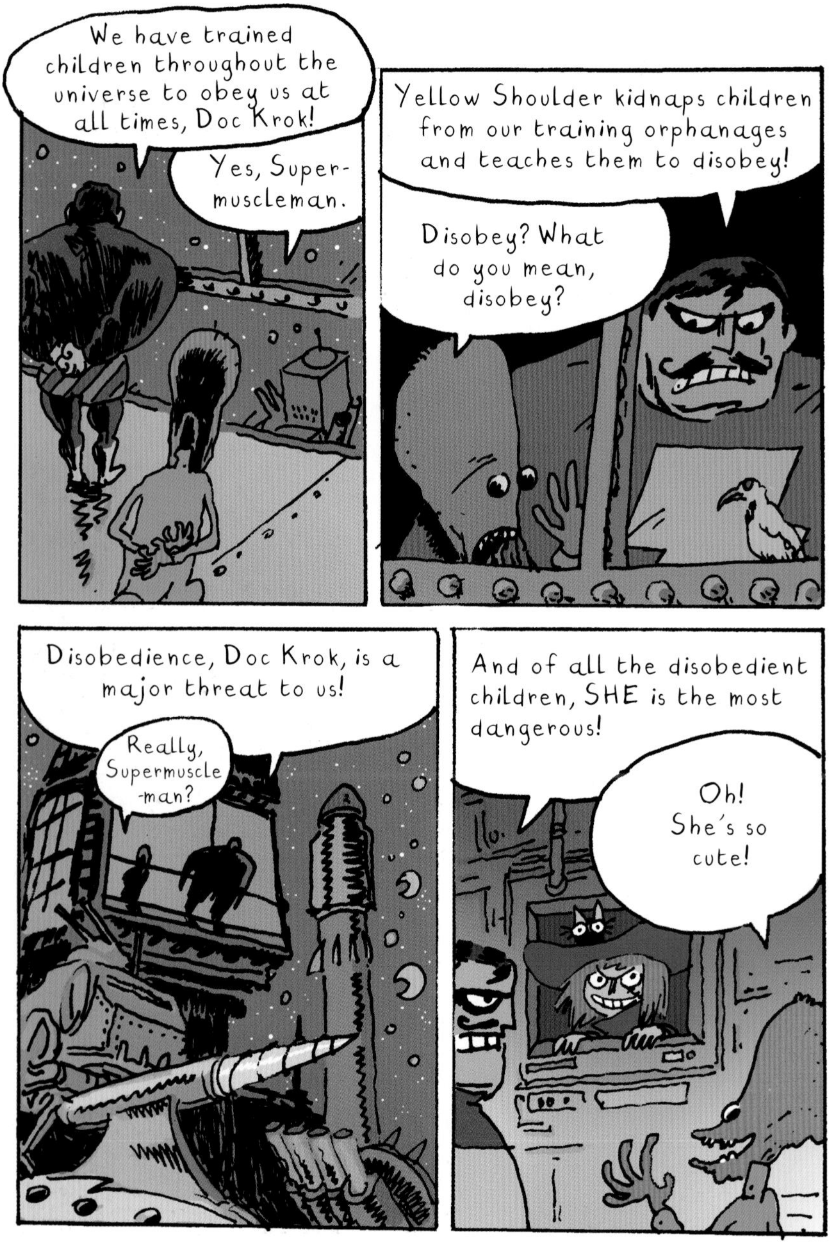
We have trained children throughout the universe to obey us at all times, Doc Krok!
Yes, Supermuscleman.
Yellow Shoulder kidnaps children from our training orphanages and teaches them to disobey!
Disobey? What do you mean, disobey?
Disobedience, Doc Krok, is a major threat to us!
Really, Supermuscle-man?
And of all the disobedient children, SHE is the most dangerous!
Oh! She's so cute!

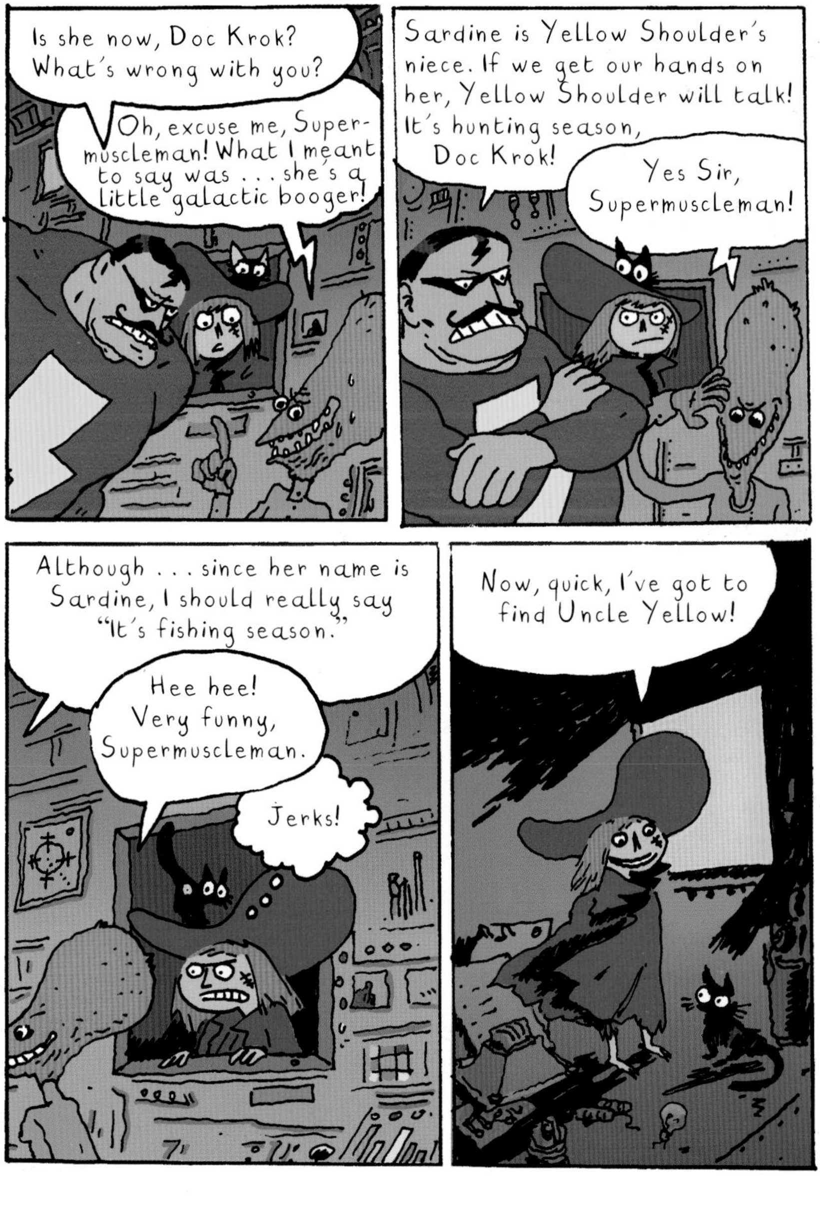
Is she now, Doc Krok? What's wrong with you?
Oh, excuse me, Supermuscleman! What I meant to say was . . . she's a little galactic booger!
Sardine is Yellow Shoulder's niece. If we get our hands on her, Yellow Shoulder will talk! It's hunting season, Doc Krok!
Yes Sir, Supermuscleman!
Although . . . since her name is Sardine, I should really say "It's fishing season."
Hee hee! Very funny, Supermuscleman.
Jerks!
Now, quick, I've got to find Uncle Yellow!

He must be on one of these monitors . . .

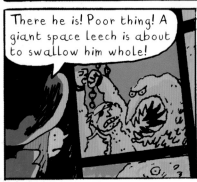

There he is! Poor thing! A giant space leech is about to swallow him whole!

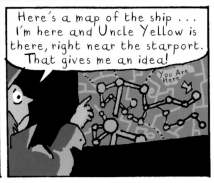

Here's a map of the ship . . . I'm here and Uncle Yellow is there, right near the starport. That gives me an idea!

You Are Here

Change of plans, Yellow Shoulder. We're going after your niece!

Sardine? You'll have to catch her first, you cosmic spitwad!

That's right! Just you try and catch me, Doc Krok!

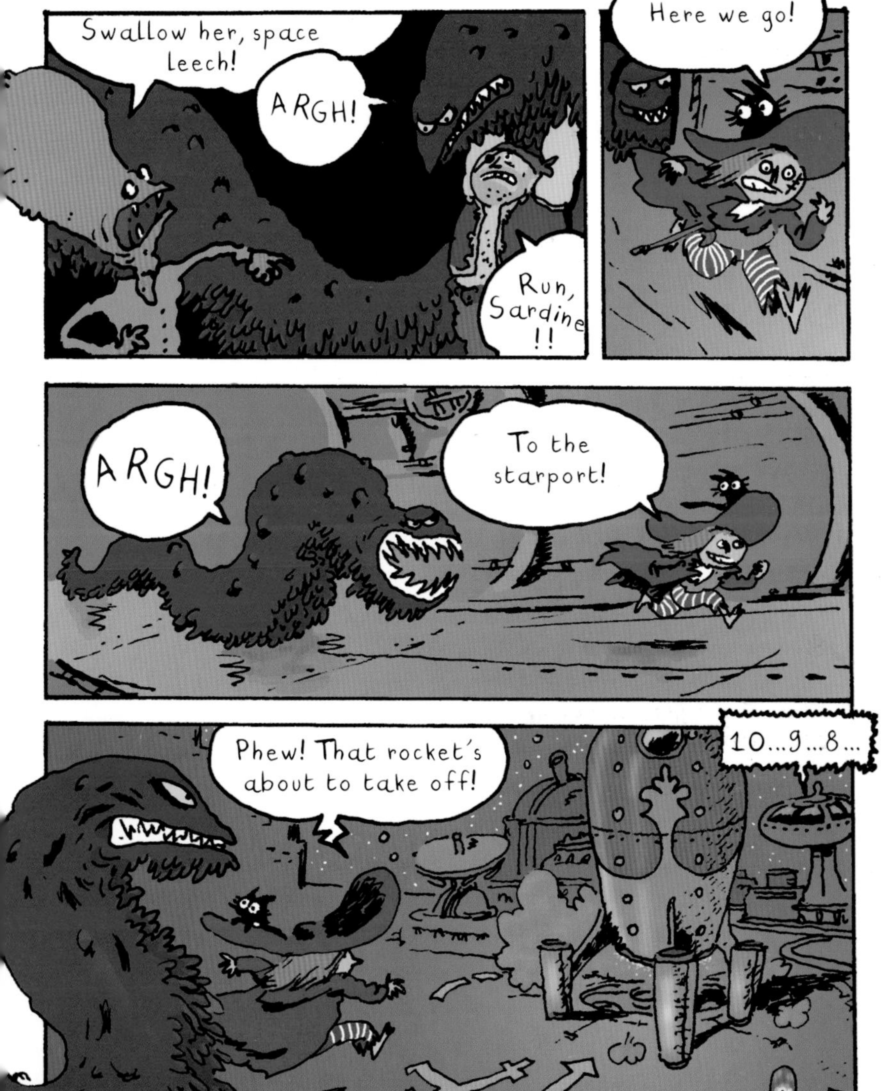
Swallow her, space leech!
ARGH!
Run, Sardine!!
Here we go!
ARGH!
To the starport!
Phew! That rocket's about to take off!
10...9...8...

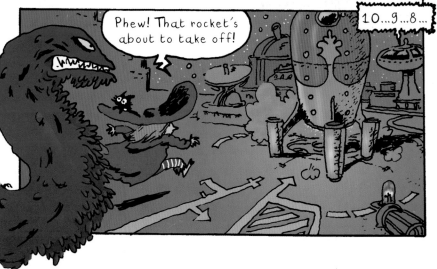

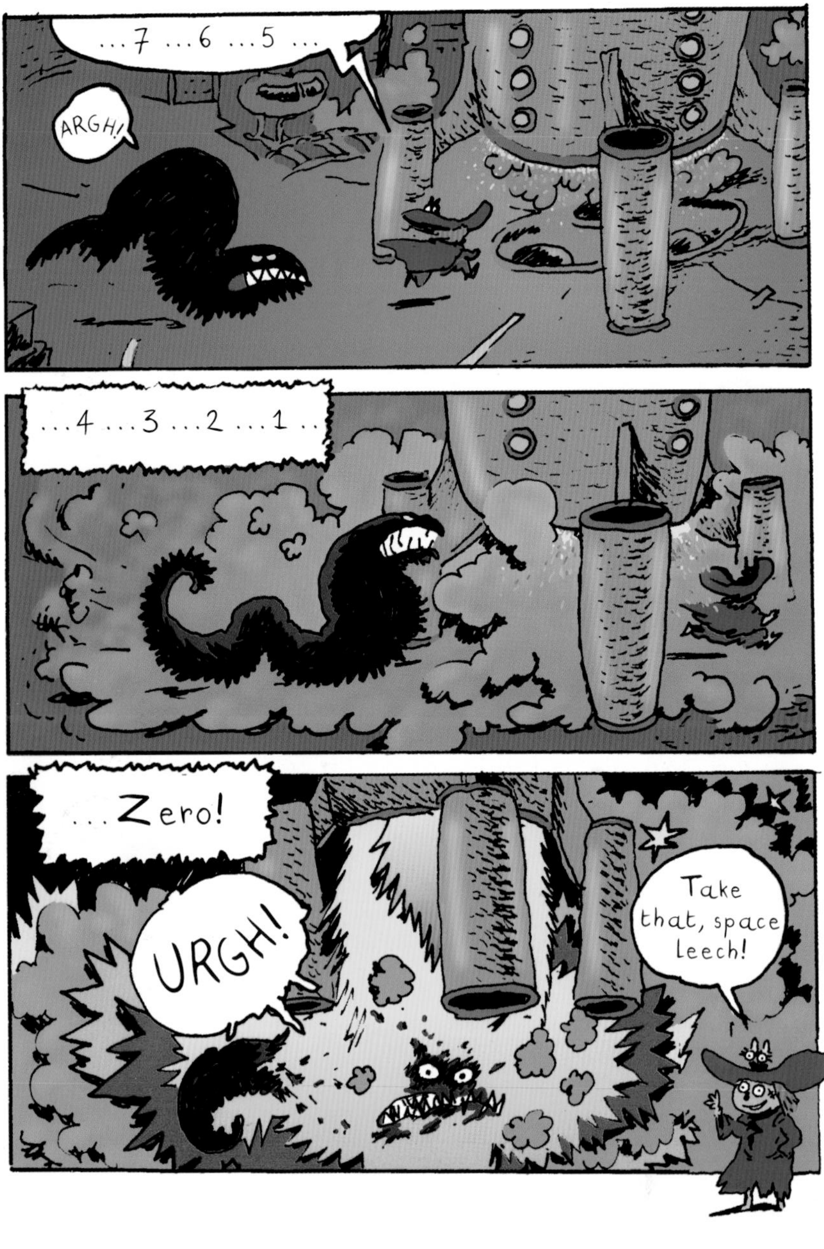
...7 ...6 ...5 ...
ARGH!
...4 ...3 ...2 ...1 ...
...Zero!
URGH!
Take that, space leech!

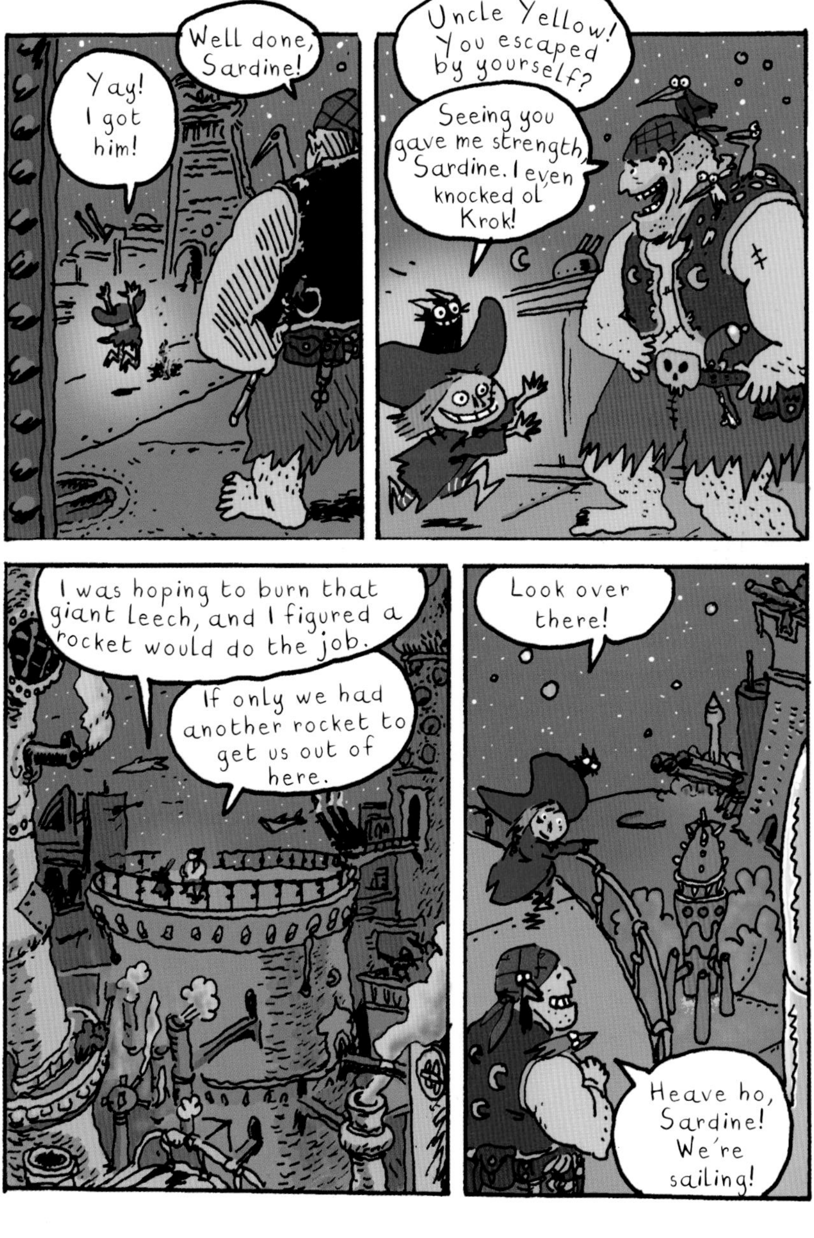
Well done, Sardine!
Yay! I got him!
Uncle Yellow! You escaped by yourself?
Seeing you gave me strength, Sardine. I even knocked ol' Krok!
I was hoping to burn that giant leech, and I figured a rocket would do the job.
If only we had another rocket to get us out of here.
Look over there!
Heave ho, Sardine! We're sailing!

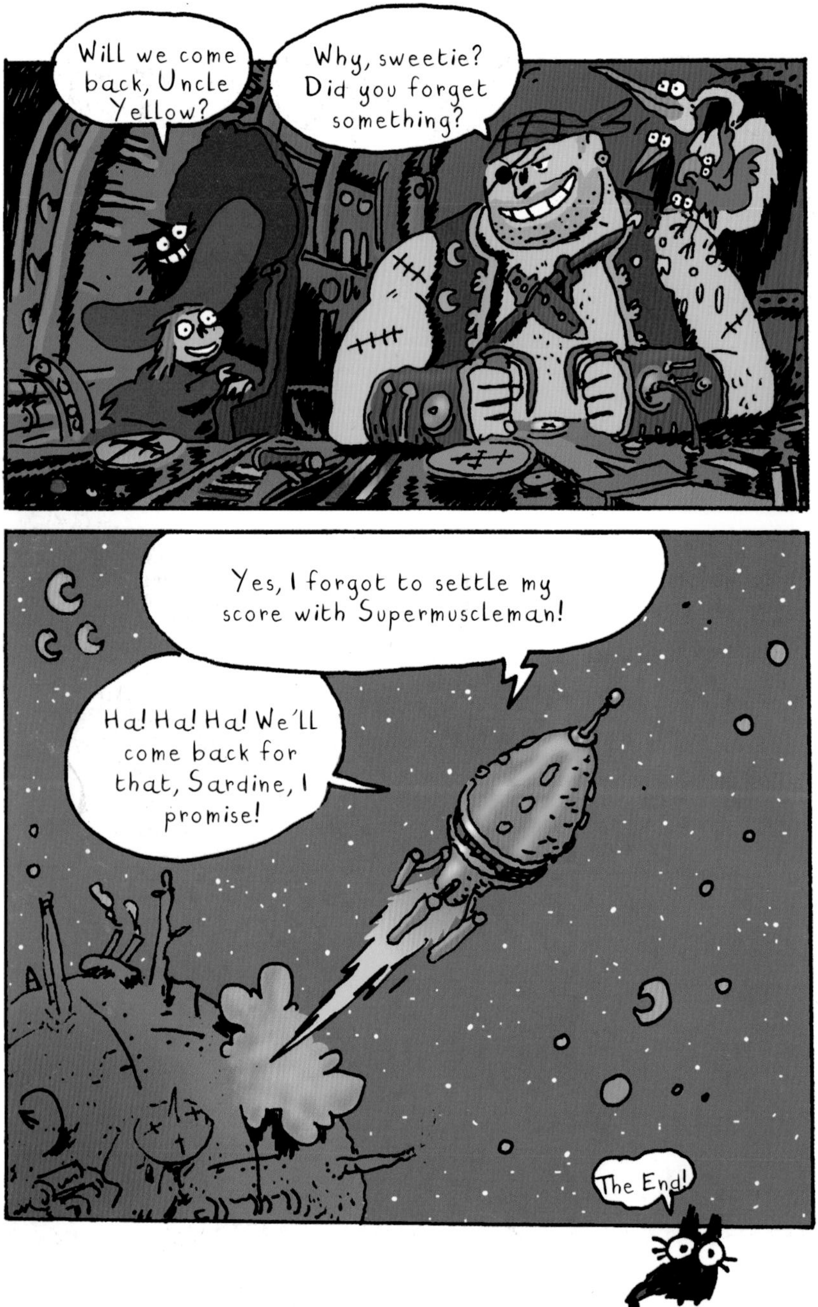
Will we come back, Uncle Yellow?
Why, sweetie? Did you forget something?
Yes, I forgot to settle my score with Supermuscleman!
Ha! Ha! Ha! We'll come back for that, Sardine, I promise!
The End!

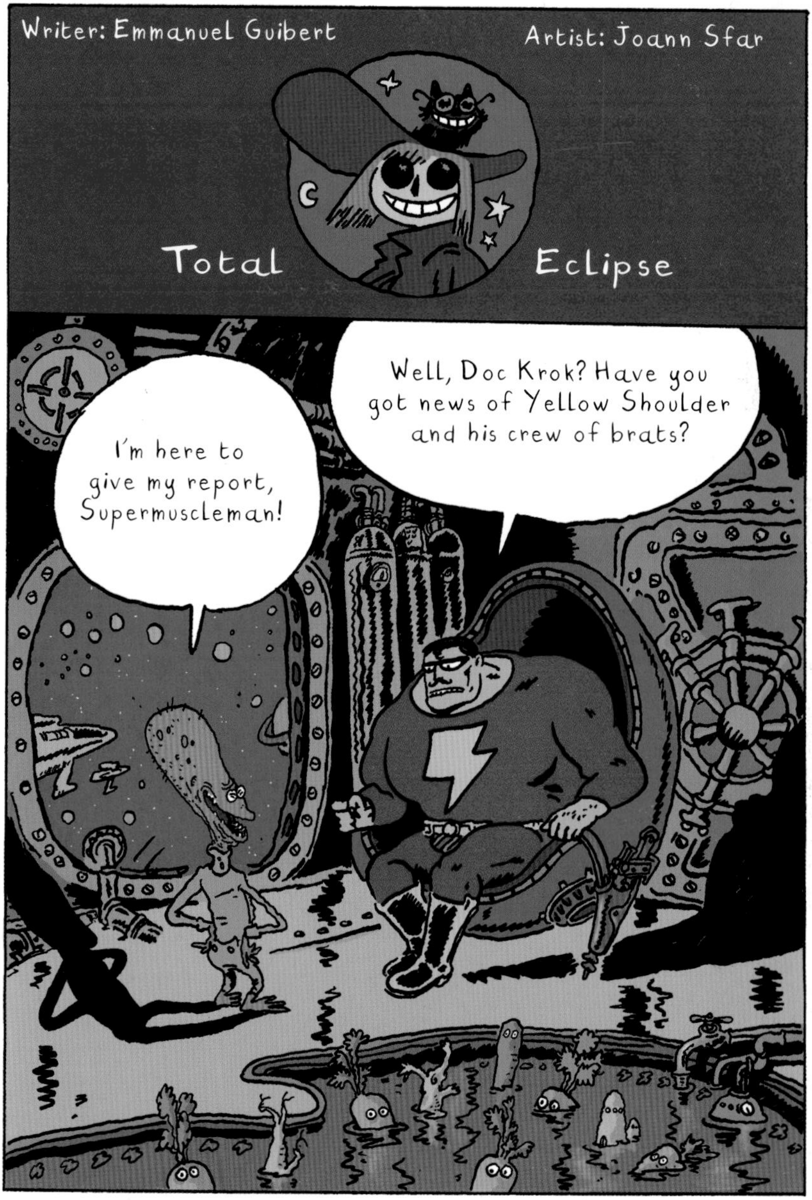

Writer: Emmanuel Guibert
Artist: Joann Sfar
Total Eclipse
Well, Doc Krok? Have you got news of Yellow Shoulder and his crew of brats?
I'm here to give my report, Supermuscleman!

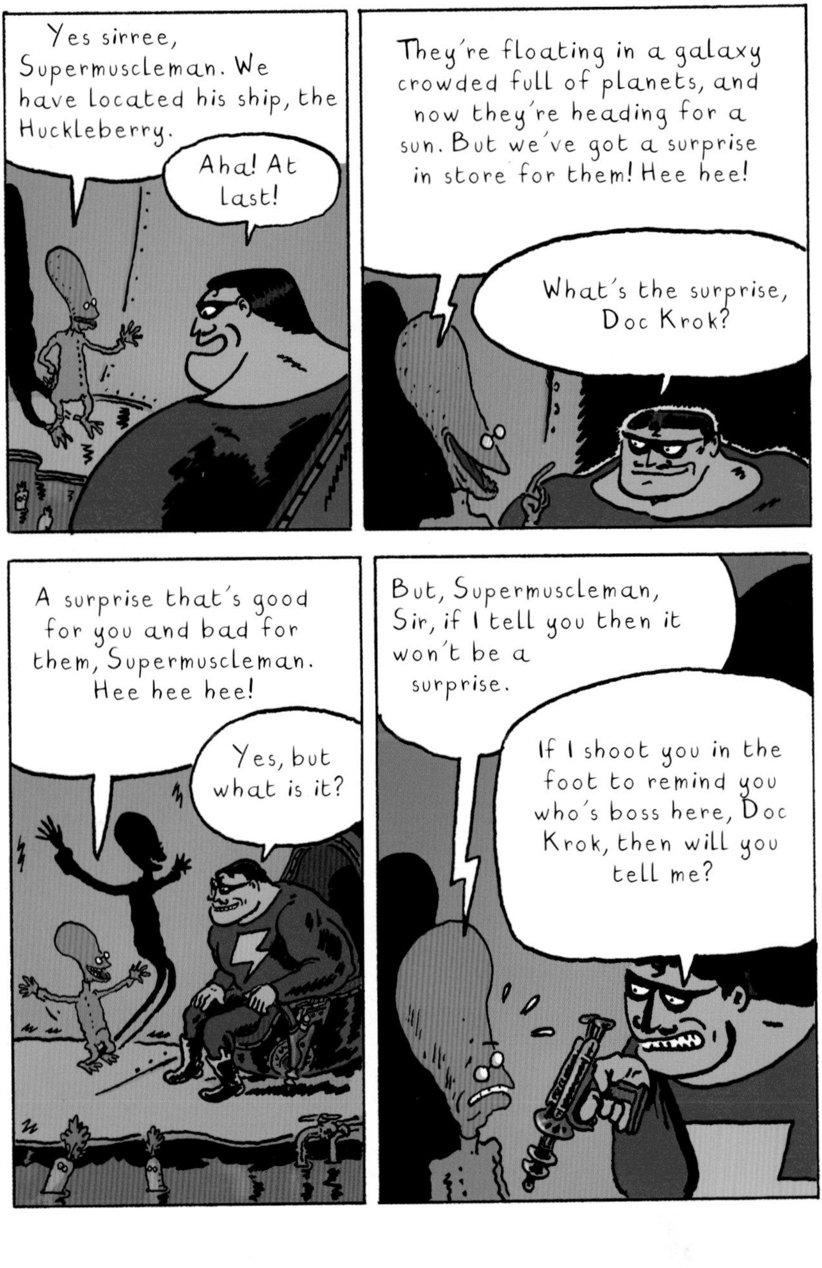
Yes sirree, Supermuscleman. We have located his ship, the Huckleberry.
Aha! At last!
They're floating in a galaxy crowded full of planets, and now they're heading for a sun. But we've got a surprise in store for them! Hee hee!
What's the surprise, Doc Krok?
A surprise that's good for you and bad for them, Supermuscleman. Hee hee hee!
Yes, but what is it?
But, Supermuscleman, Sir, if I tell you then it won't be a surprise.
If I shoot you in the foot to remind you who's boss here, Doc Krok, then will you tell me?

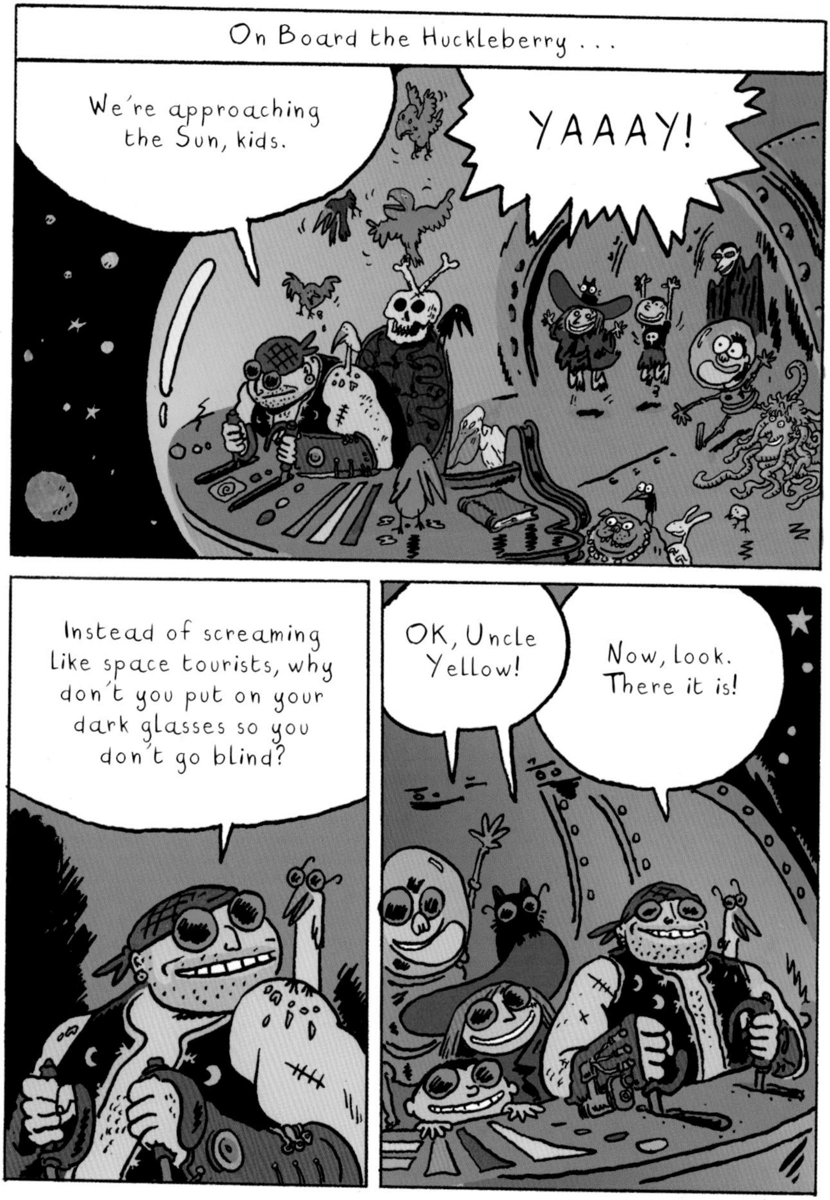
On Board the Huckleberry . . .
We're approaching the Sun, kids.
YAAAY!
Instead of screaming like space tourists, why don't you put on your dark glasses so you don't go blind?
OK, Uncle Yellow!
Now, look. There it is!

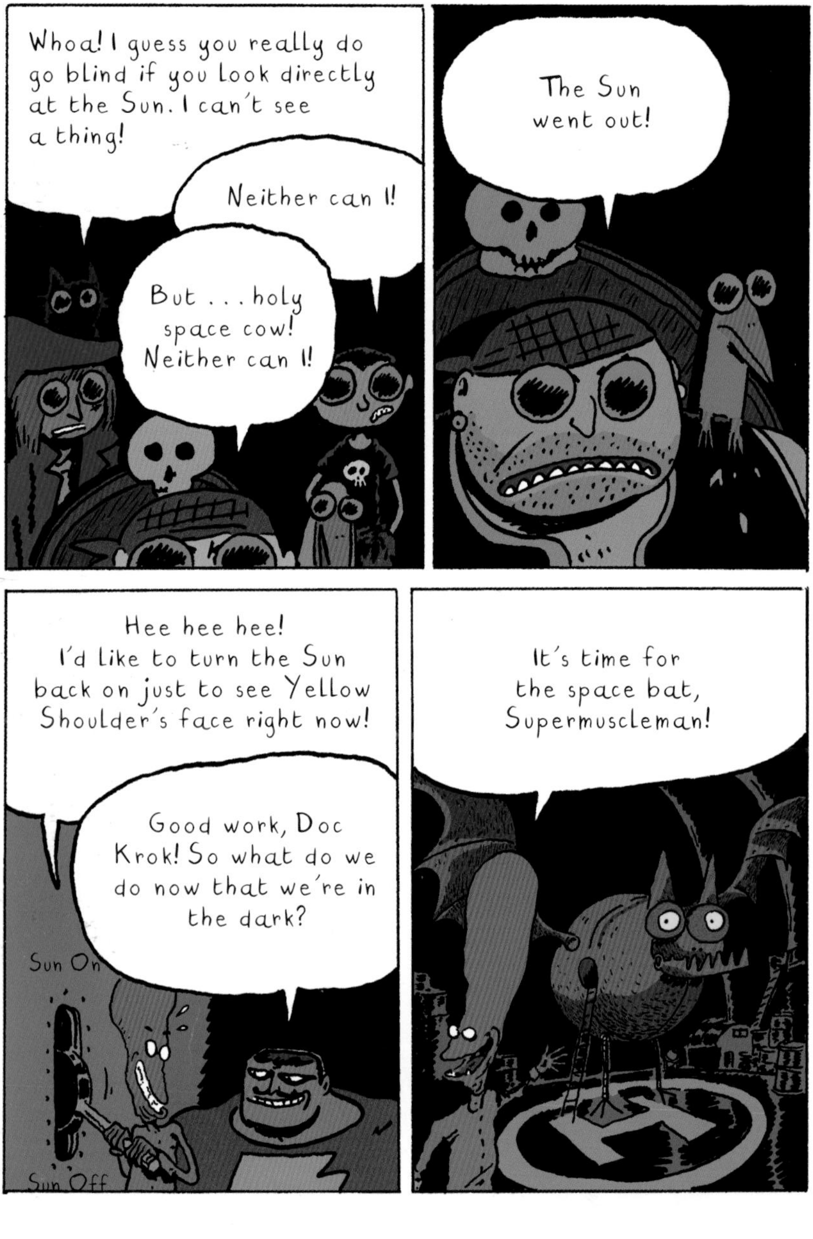
Whoa! I guess you really do go blind if you look directly at the Sun. I can't see a thing!
Neither can I!
But . . . holy space cow! Neither can I!
The Sun went out!
Hee hee hee! I'd like to turn the Sun back on just to see Yellow Shoulder's face right now!
Good work, Doc Krok! So what do we do now that we're in the dark?
Sun On
Sun Off
It's time for the space bat, Supermuscleman!

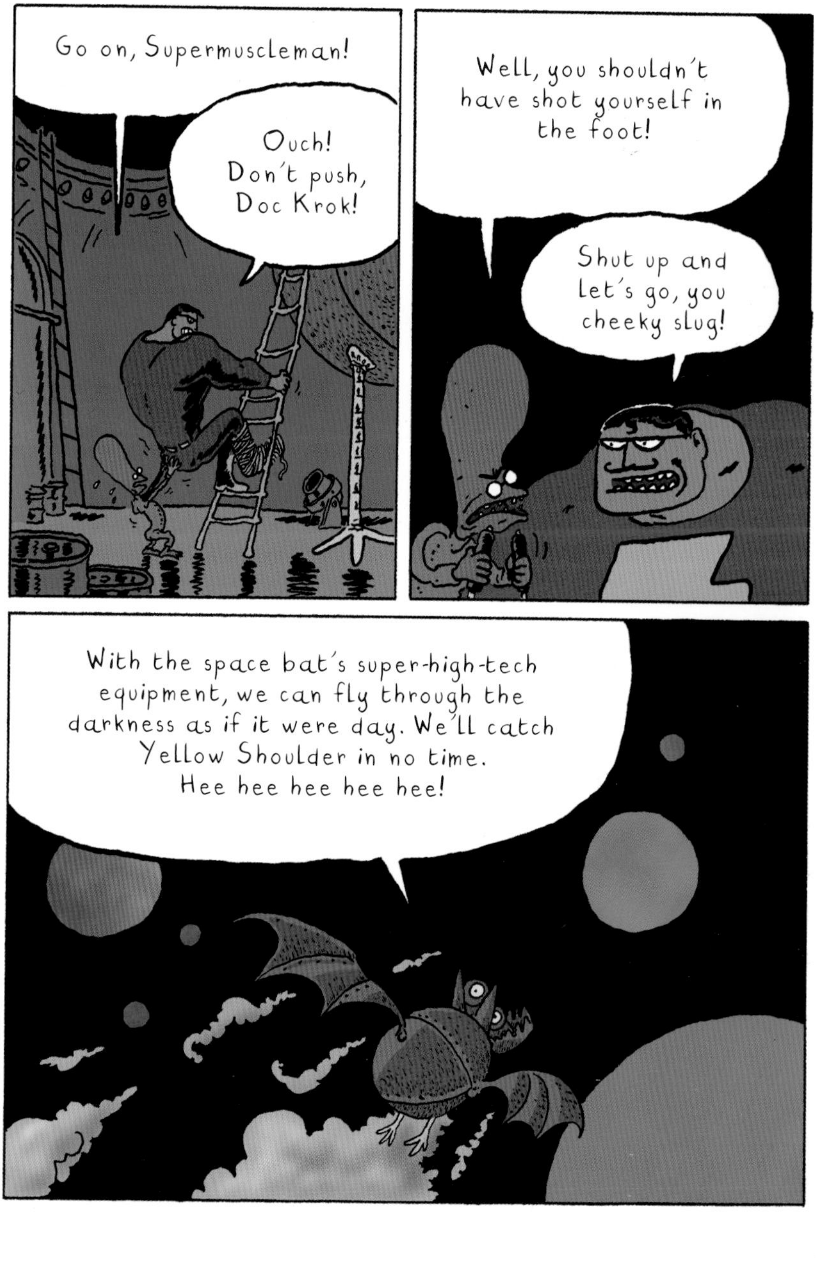
Go on, Supermuscleman!
Ouch! Don't push, Doc Krok!
Well, you shouldn't have shot yourself in the foot!
Shut up and let's go, you cheeky slug!
With the space bat's super-high-tech equipment, we can fly through the darkness as if it were day. We'll catch Yellow Shoulder in no time. Hee hee hee hee hee!

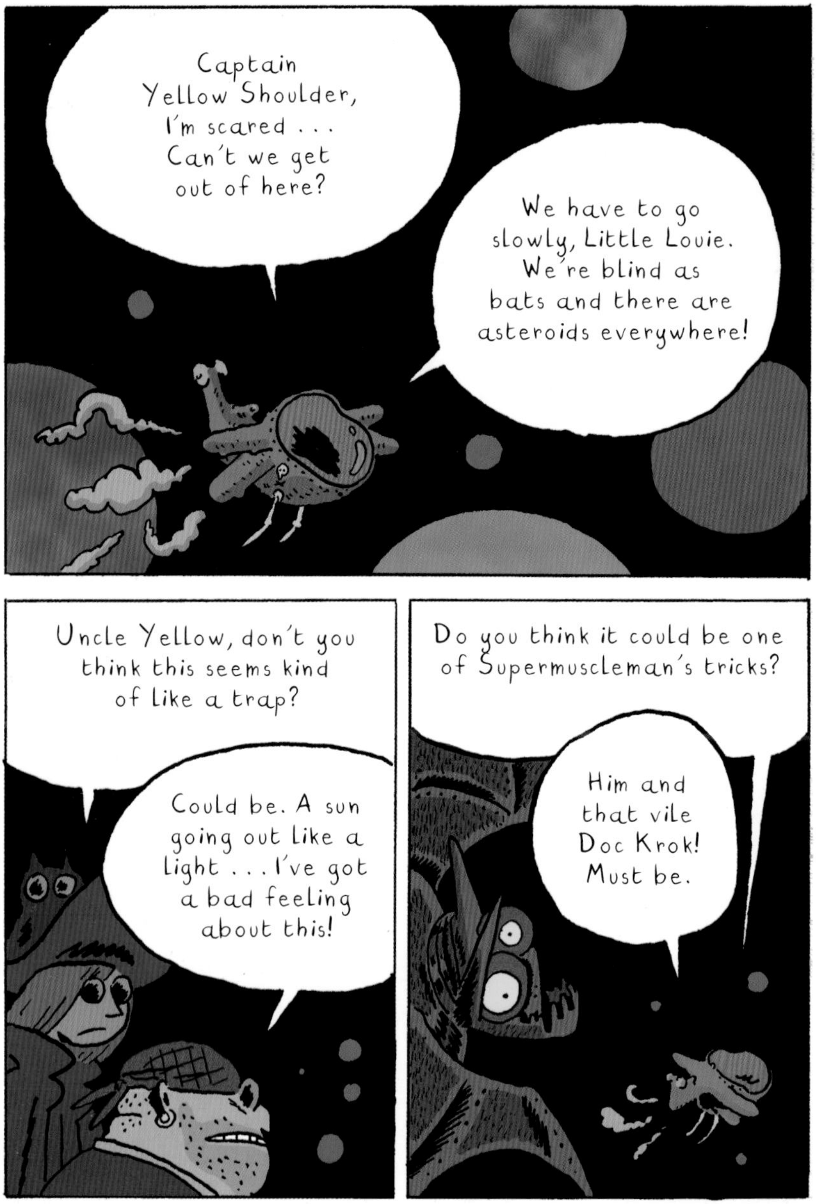
Captain Yellow Shoulder, I'm scared . . . Can't we get out of here?
We have to go slowly, Little Louie. We're blind as bats and there are asteroids everywhere!
Uncle Yellow, don't you think this seems kind of like a trap?
Could be. A sun going out like a light . . . I've got a bad feeling about this!
Do you think it could be one of Supermuscleman's tricks?
Him and that vile Doc Krok! Must be.

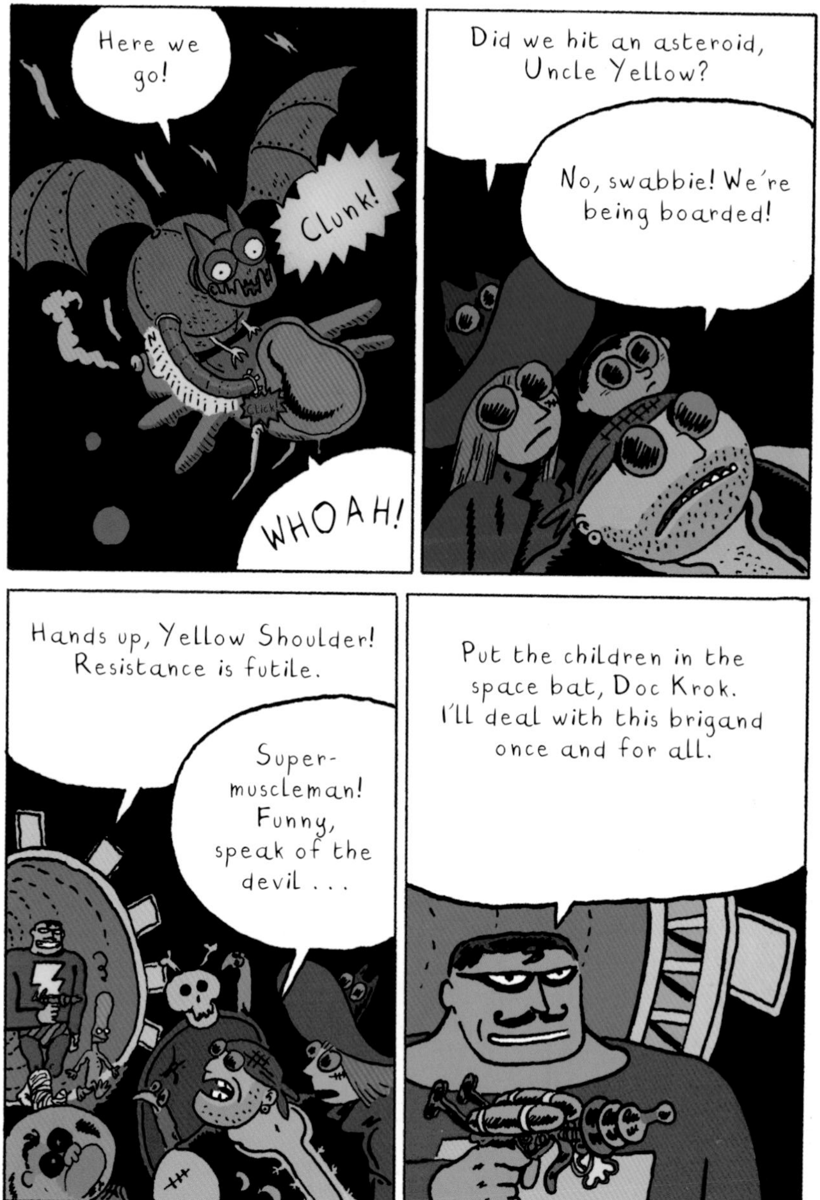
Here we go!
Clunk!
Click!
WHOAH!
Did we hit an asteroid, Uncle Yellow?
No, swabbie! We're being boarded!
Hands up, Yellow Shoulder! Resistance is futile.
Super-muscleman! Funny, speak of the devil . . .
Put the children in the space bat, Doc Krok. I'll deal with this brigand once and for all.

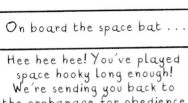

On board the space bat . . .

Hee hee hee! You've played space hooky long enough! We're sending you back to the orphanage for obedience training, back where you belong!

I doubt you can be broken, Sardine. Better just throw you out into space. Hee hee hee!

Please, one final request!

What, then?

Well, I always learned that you should turn out the light when you leave a room, but this time . . .

Sun

...I'M TURNING IT ON!

Click!

Sun On

Sun Off

20

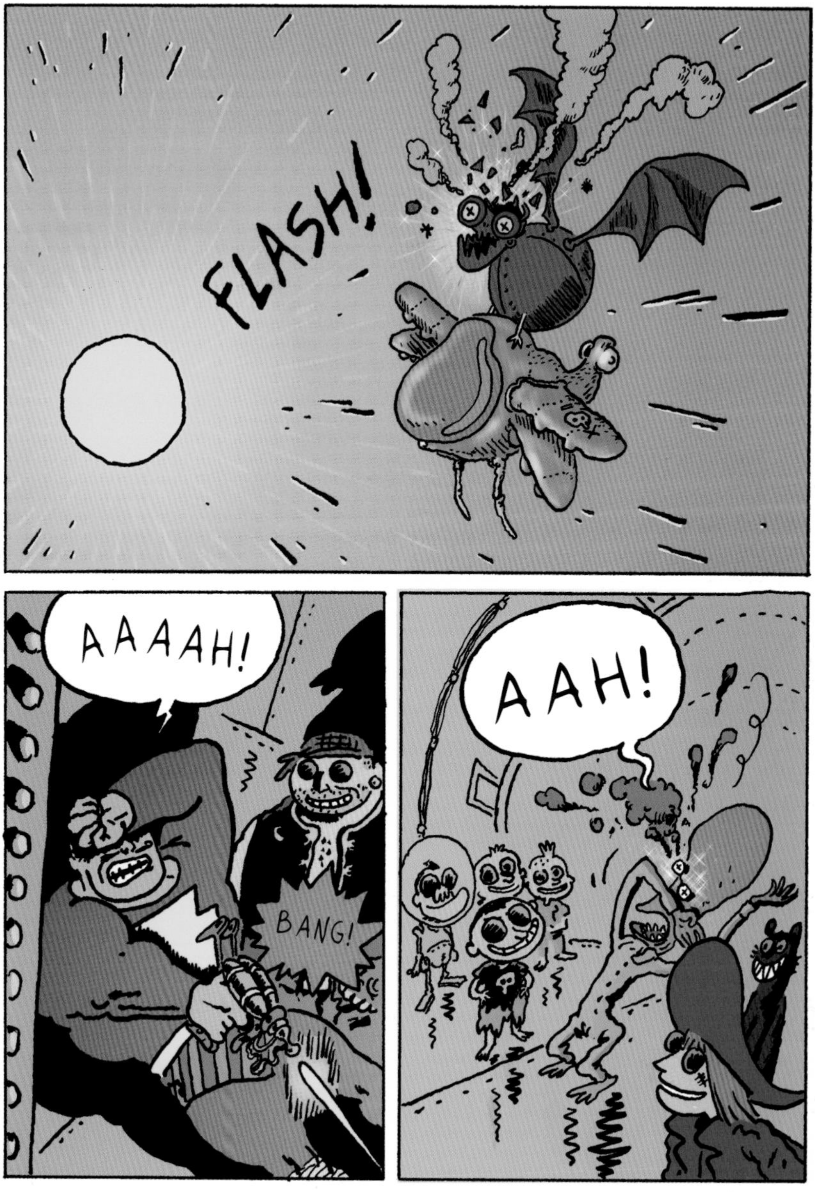
FLASH!
AAAAH!
BANG!
AAH!

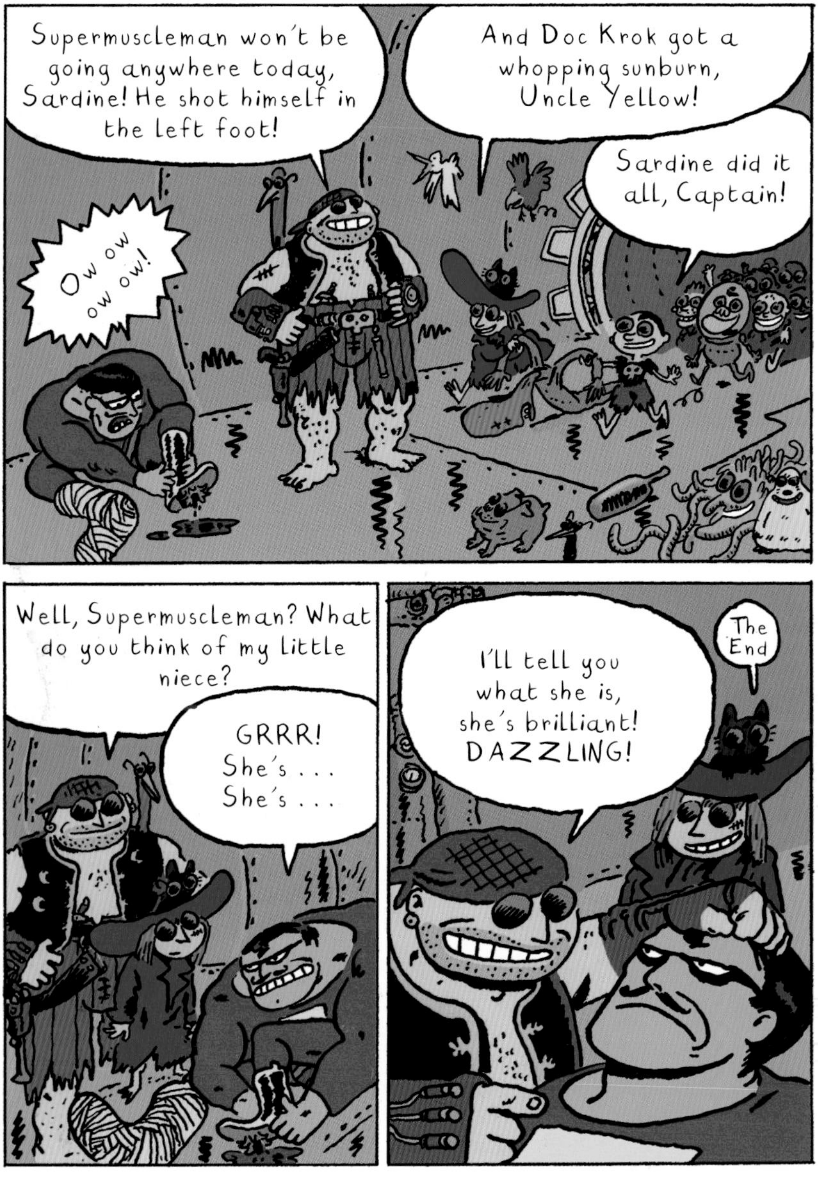
Supermuscleman won't be going anywhere today, Sardine! He shot himself in the left foot!
Ow ow ow ow!
And Doc Krok got a whopping sunburn, Uncle Yellow!
Sardine did it all, Captain!
Well, Supermuscleman? What do you think of my little niece?
GRRR! She's . . . She's . . .
I'll tell you what she is, she's brilliant! DAZZLING!
The End

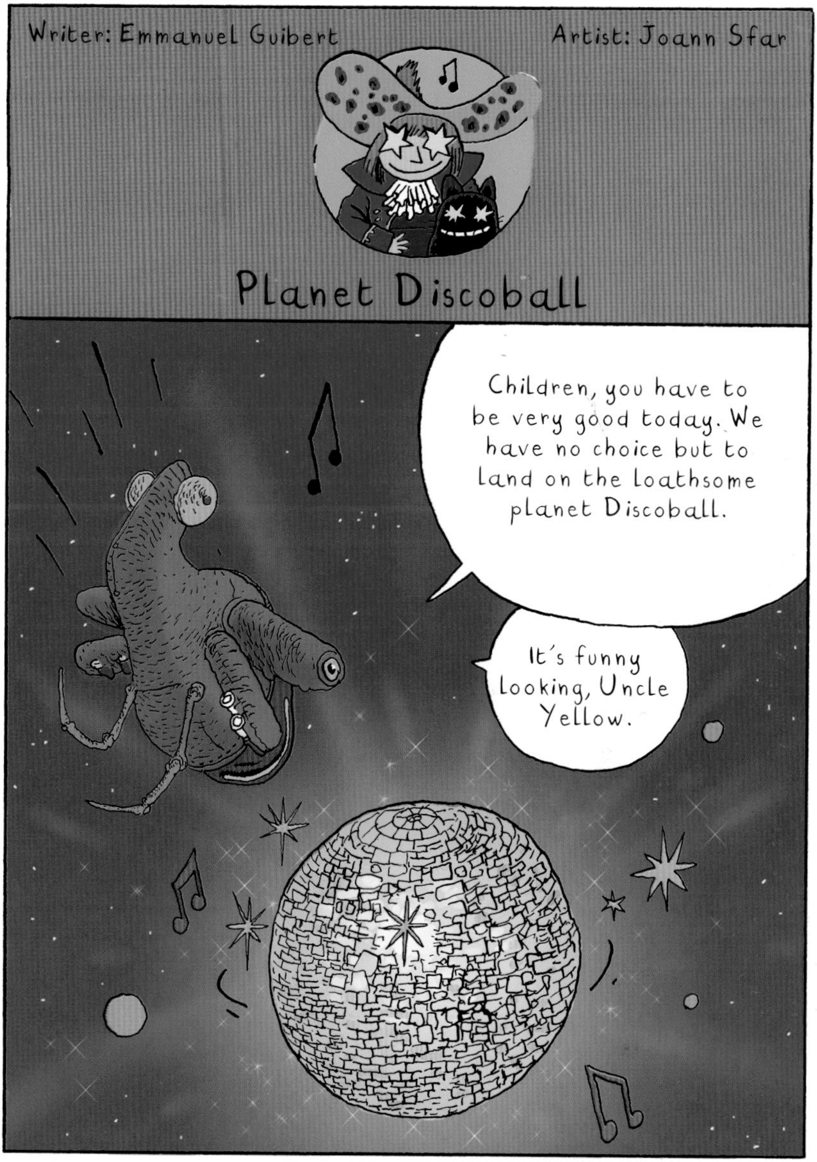
Writer: Emmanuel Guibert
Artist: Joann Sfar
Planet Discoball
Children, you have to be very good today. We have no choice but to land on the loathsome planet Discoball.
It's funny looking, Uncle Yellow.

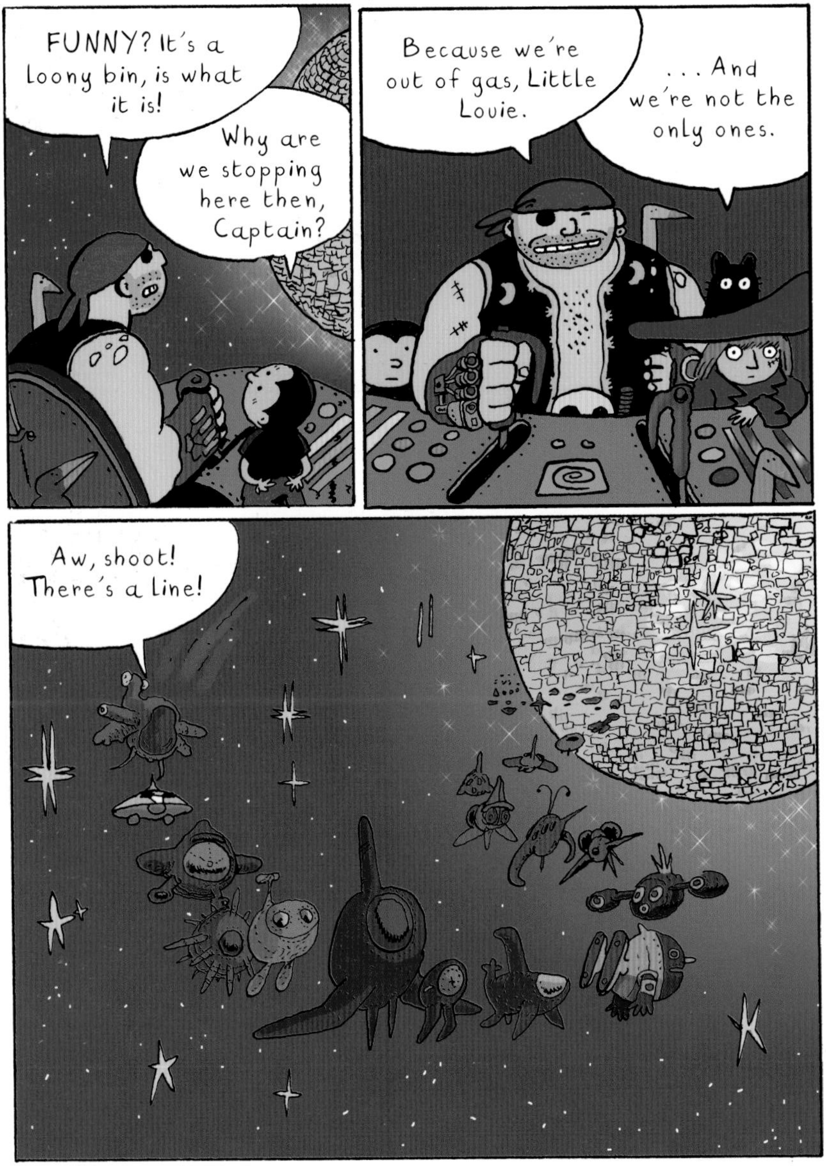
FUNNY? It's a loony bin, is what it is!
Why are we stopping here then, Captain?
Because we're out of gas, Little Louie.
...And we're not the only ones.
Aw, shoot! There's a line!

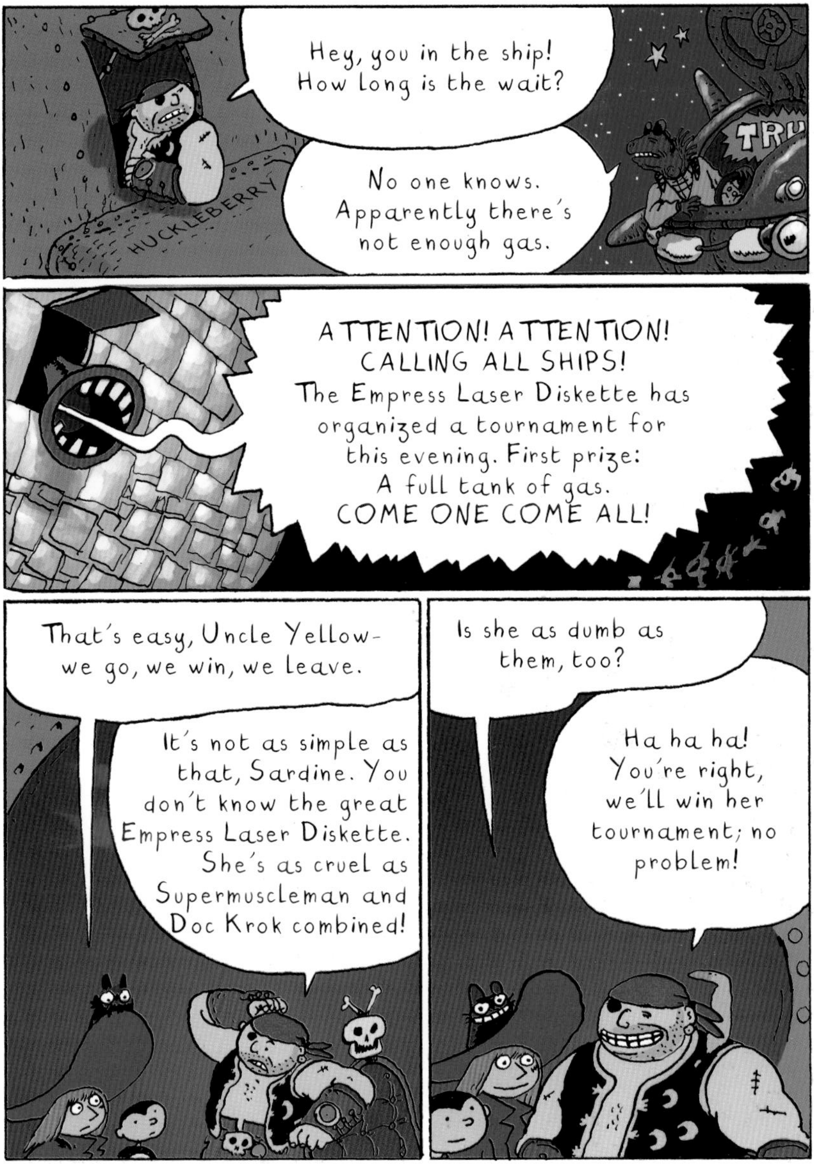
Hey, you in the ship! How long is the wait?
No one knows. Apparently there's not enough gas.
HUCKLEBERRY
ATTENTION! ATTENTION! CALLING ALL SHIPS! The Empress Laser Diskette has organized a tournament for this evening. First prize: A full tank of gas. COME ONE COME ALL!
That's easy, Uncle Yellow-we go, we win, we leave.
It's not as simple as that, Sardine. You don't know the great Empress Laser Diskette. She's as cruel as Supermuscleman and Doc Krok combined!
Is she as dumb as them, too?
Ha ha ha! You're right, we'll win her tournament; no problem!

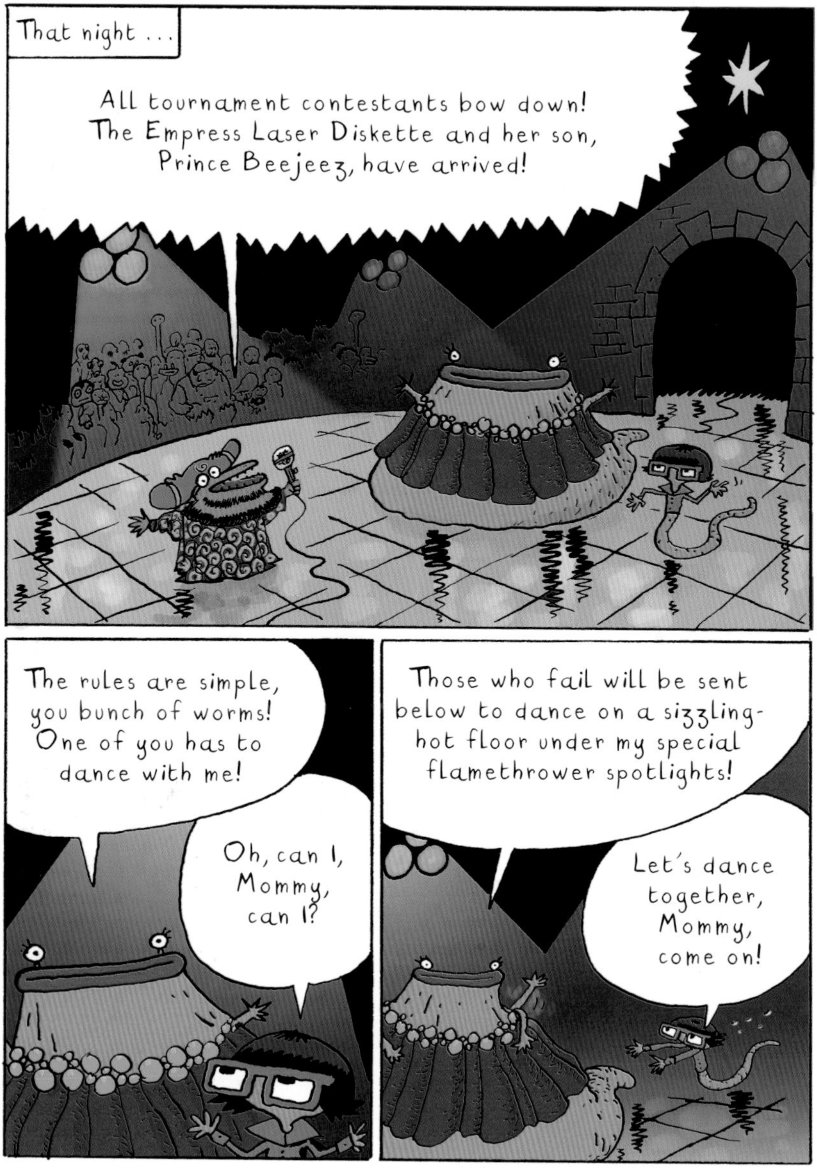
That night . . .
All tournament contestants bow down! The Empress Laser Diskette and her son, Prince Beejeez, have arrived!
The rules are simple, you bunch of worms! One of you has to dance with me!
Oh, can I, Mommy, can I?
Those who fail will be sent below to dance on a sizzling-hot floor under my special flamethrower spotlights!
Let's dance together, Mommy, come on!

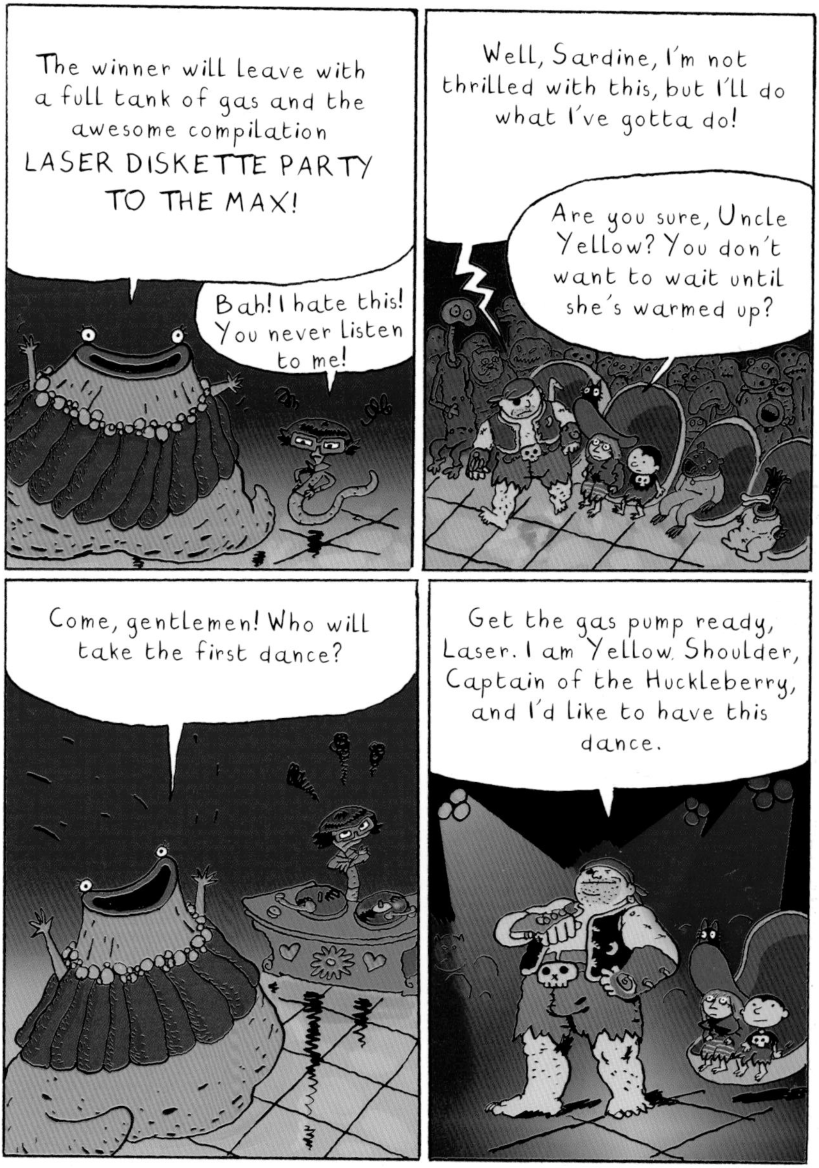
The winner will leave with a full tank of gas and the awesome compilation LASER DISKETTE PARTY TO THE MAX!
Bah! I hate this! You never listen to me!
Well, Sardine, I'm not thrilled with this, but I'll do what I've gotta do!
Are you sure, Uncle Yellow? You don't want to wait until she's warmed up?
Come, gentlemen! Who will take the first dance?
Get the gas pump ready, Laser. I am Yellow Shoulder, Captain of the Huckleberry, and I'd like to have this dance.

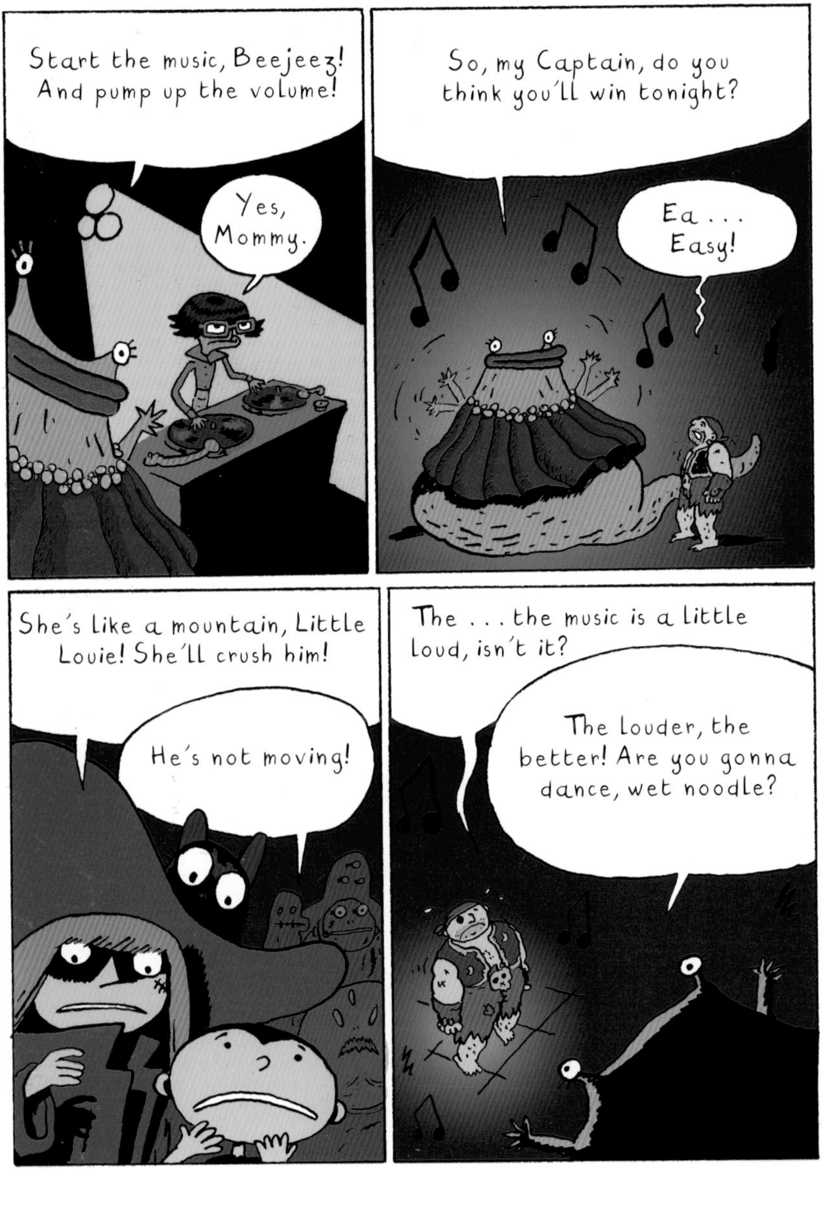
Start the music, Beejeez! And pump up the volume!
Yes, Mommy.
So, my Captain, do you think you'll win tonight?
Ea . . . Easy!
She's like a mountain, Little Louie! She'll crush him!
He's not moving!
The . . . the music is a little loud, isn't it?
The louder, the better! Are you gonna dance, wet noodle?

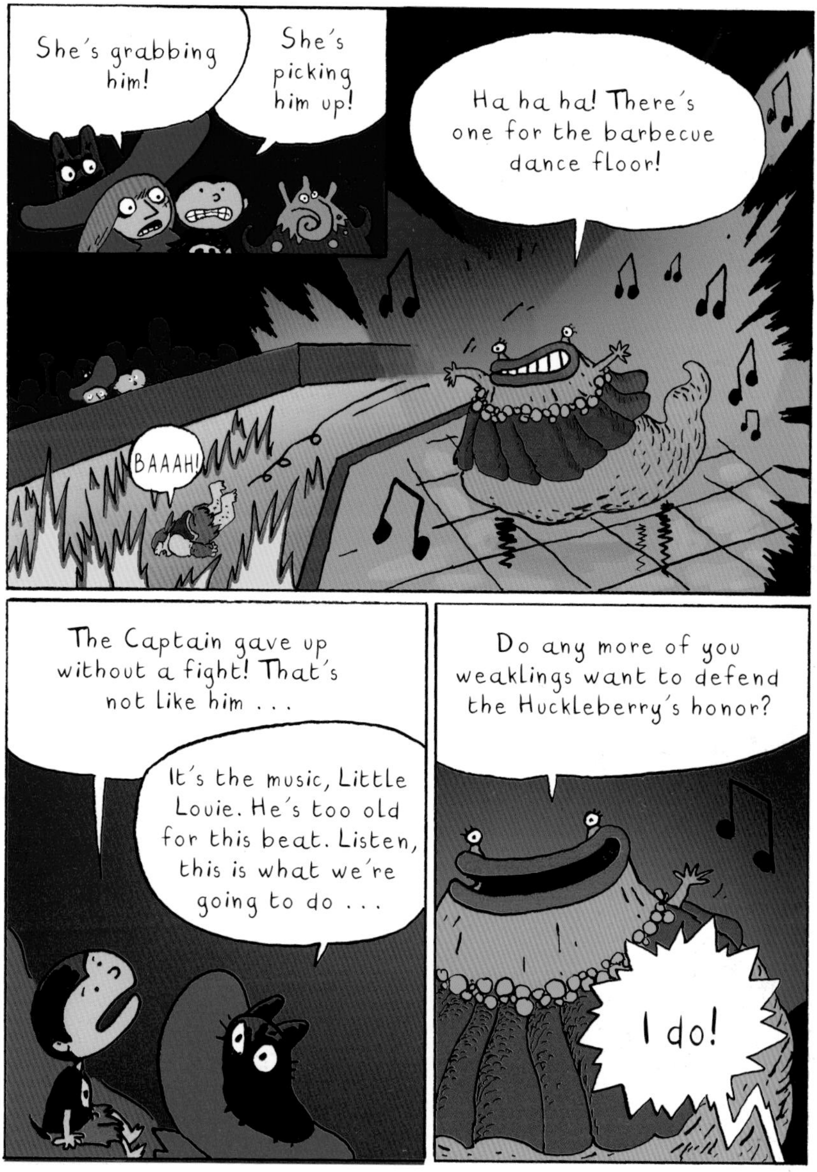
She's grabbing him!
She's picking him up!
Ha ha ha! There's one for the barbecue dance floor!
BAAAH!
The Captain gave up without a fight! That's not like him . . .
It's the music, Little Louie. He's too old for this beat. Listen, this is what we're going to do . . .
Do any more of you weaklings want to defend the Huckleberry's honor?
I do!

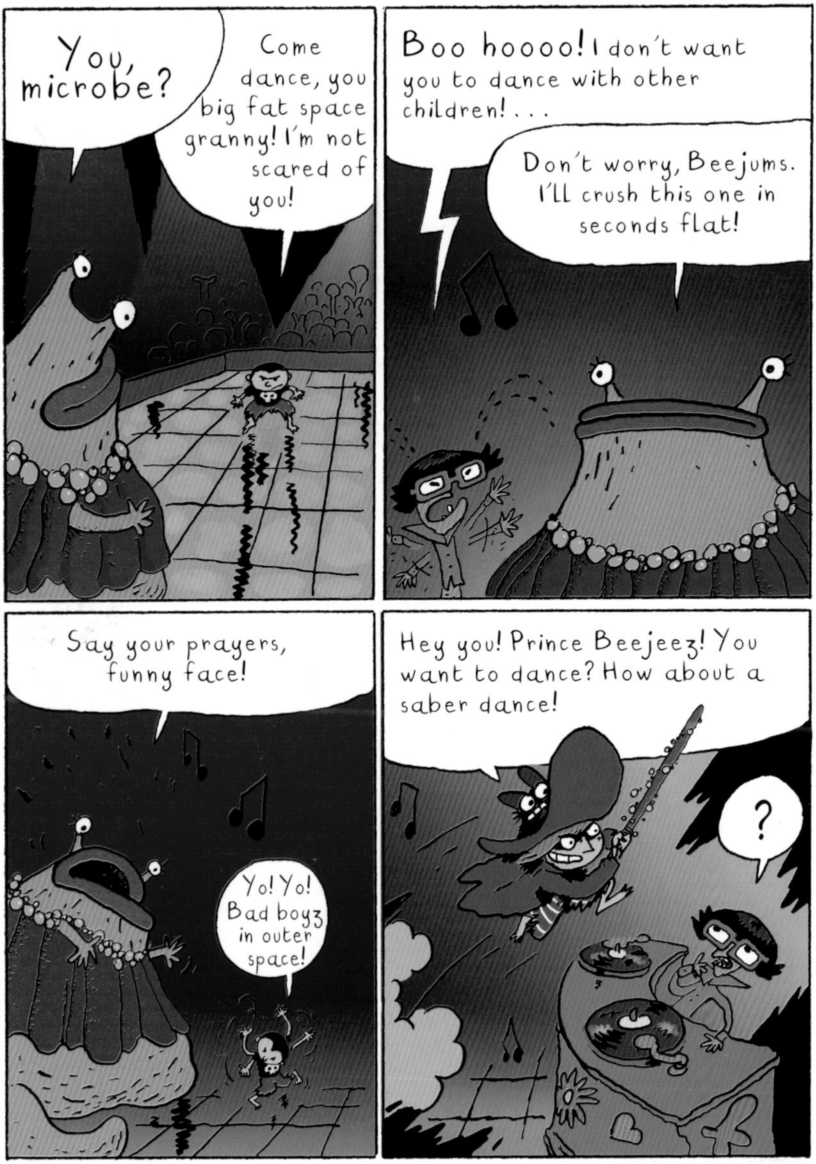
You, microbe?
Come dance, you big fat space granny! I'm not scared of you!
Boo hoooo! I don't want you to dance with other children! . . .
Don't worry, Beejums. I'll crush this one in seconds flat!
Say your prayers, funny face!
Yo! Yo! Bad boyz in outer space!
Hey you! Prince Beejeez! You want to dance? How about a saber dance!
?

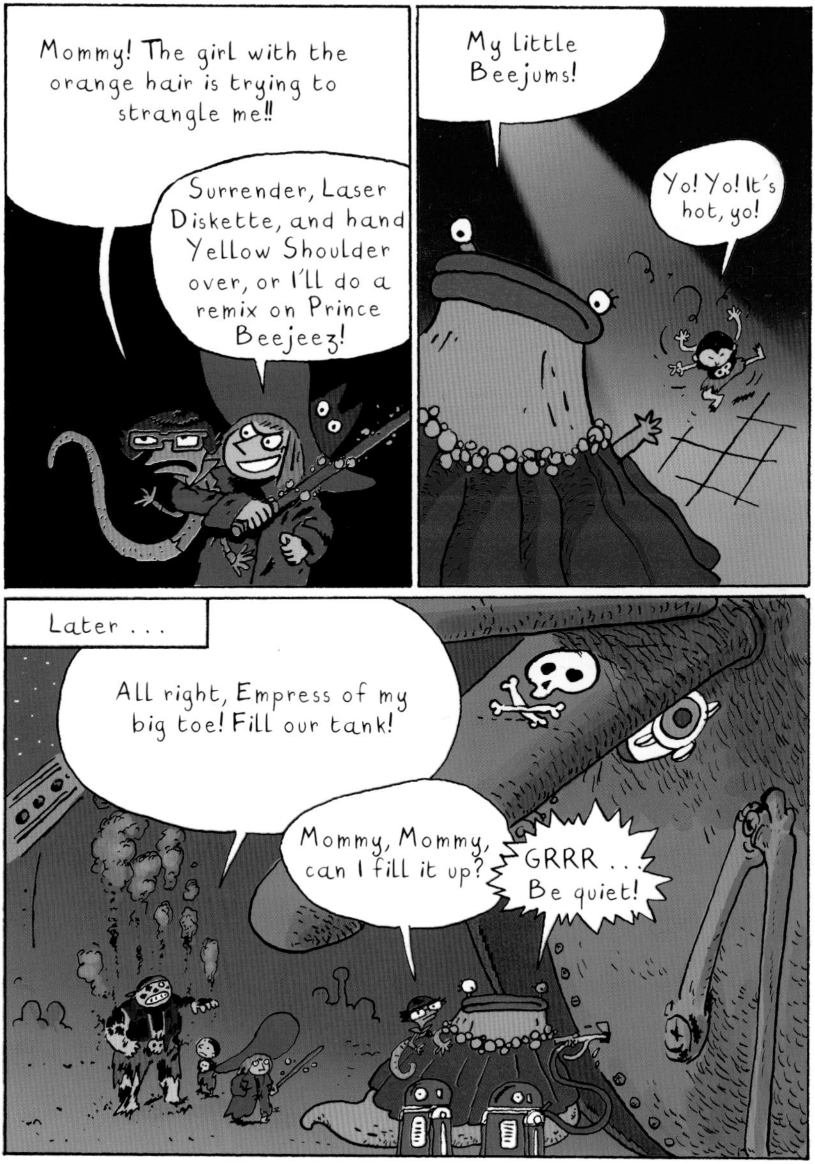
Mommy! The girl with the orange hair is trying to strangle me!!
Surrender, Laser Diskette, and hand Yellow Shoulder over, or I'll do a remix on Prince Beejeez!
My little Beejums!
Yo! Yo! It's hot, yo!
Later . . .
All right, Empress of my big toe! Fill our tank!
Mommy, Mommy, can I fill it up?
GRRR . . . Be quiet!

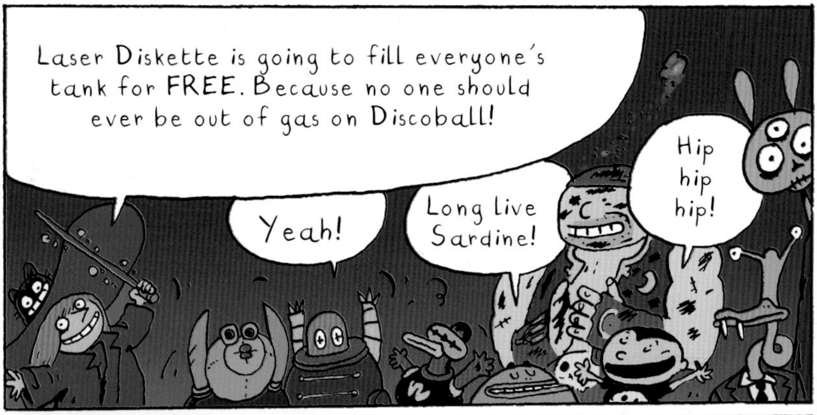
Laser Diskette is going to fill everyone's tank for FREE. Because no one should ever be out of gas on Discoball!
Yeah!
Long live Sardine!
Hip hip hip!

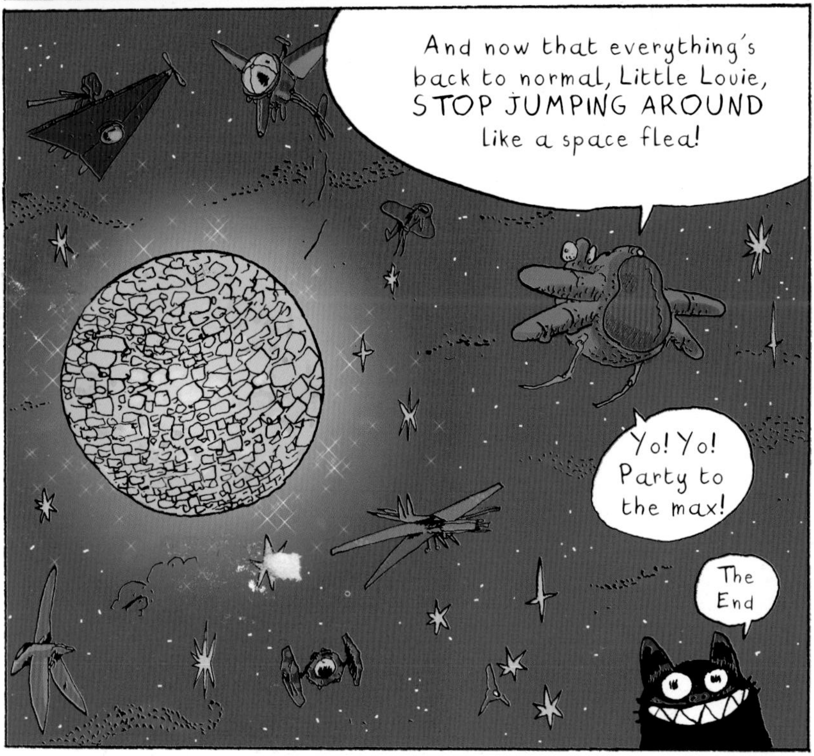
And now that everything's back to normal, Little Louie, STOP JUMPING AROUND like a space flea!
Yo! Yo! Party to the max!
The End

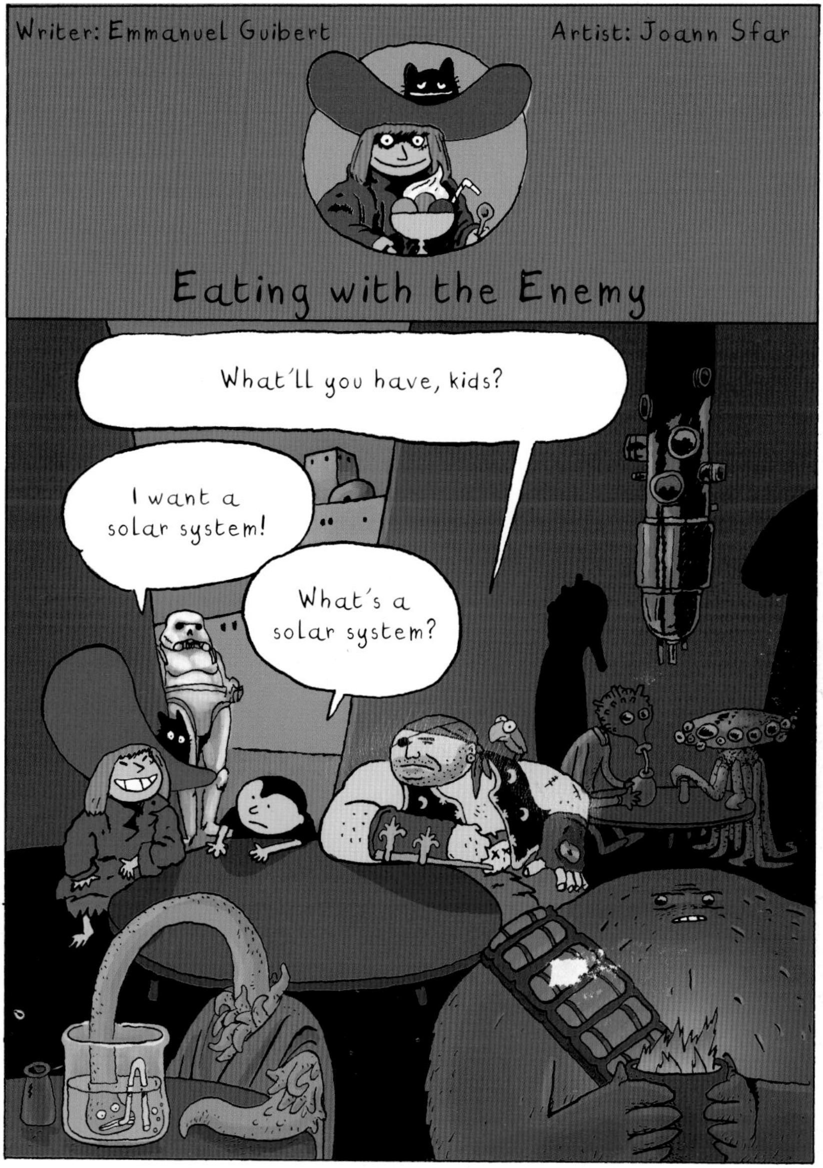
Writer: Emmanuel Guibert
Artist: Joann Sfar
Eating with the Enemy
What'll you have, kids?
I want a solar system!
What's a solar system?

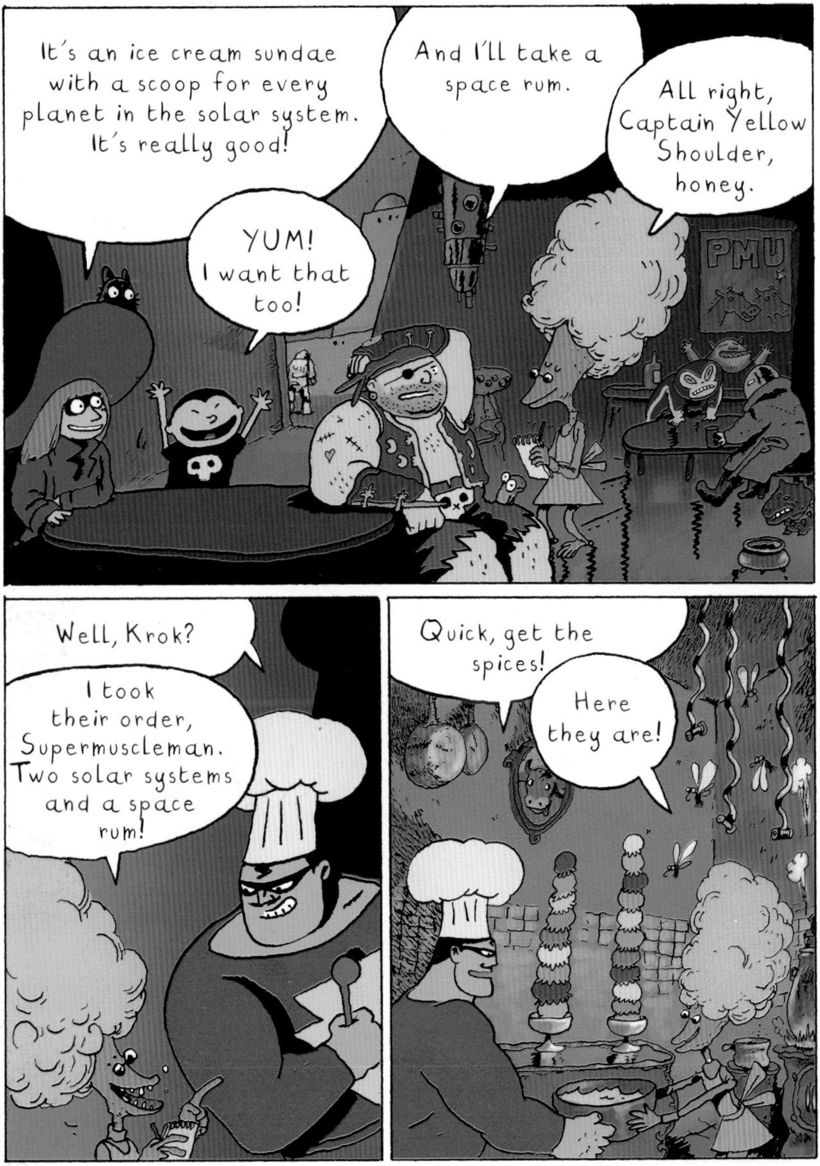
It's an ice cream sundae with a scoop for every planet in the solar system. It's really good!
YUM! I want that too!
And I'll take a space rum.
All right, Captain Yellow Shoulder, honey.
PMU
Well, Krok?
I took their order, Supermuscleman. Two solar systems and a space rum!
Quick, get the spices!
Here they are!

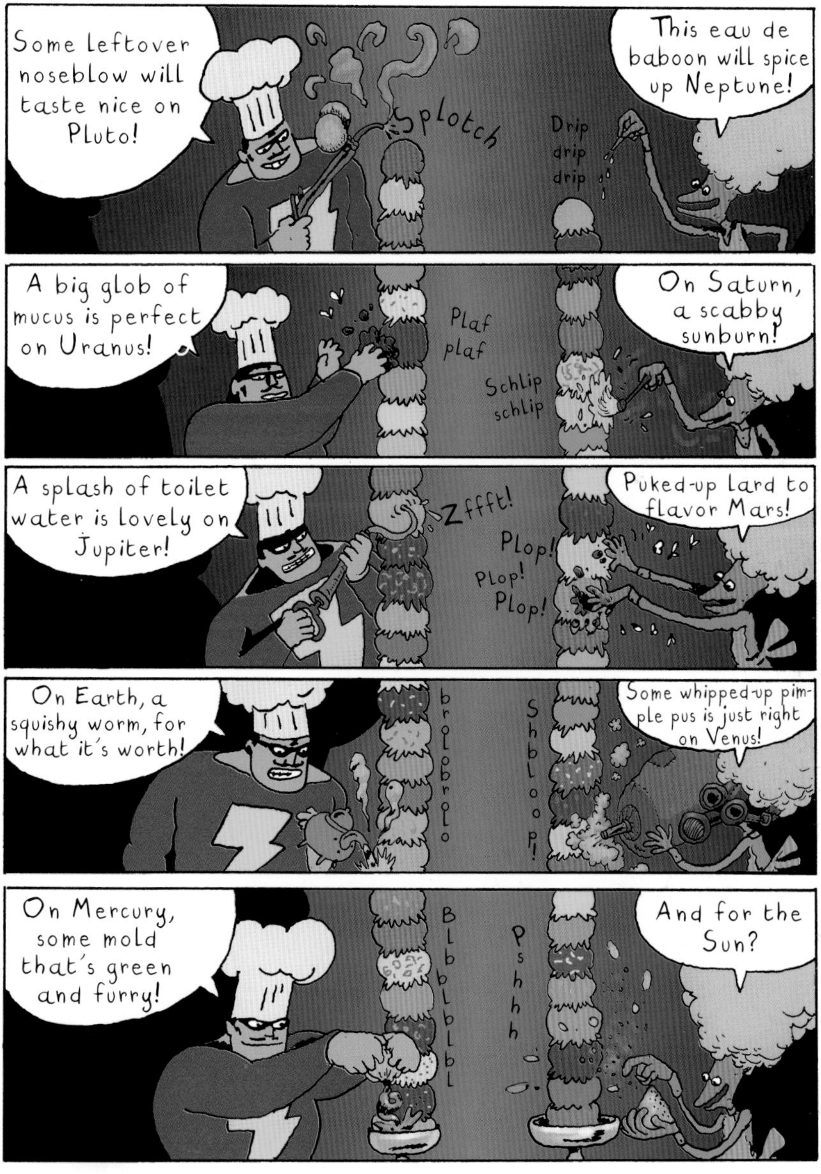
Some leftover noseblow will taste nice on Pluto!
Splotch
Drip drip drip
This eau de baboon will spice up Neptune!
A big glob of mucus is perfect on Uranus!
Plaf plaf
Schlip schlip
On Saturn, a scabby sunburn!
A splash of toilet water is lovely on Jupiter!
Zffft!
Plop! Plop! Plop!
Puked-up lard to flavor Mars!
On Earth, a squishy worm, for what it's worth!
brolobrolo
Shbloop!
Some whipped-up pimple pus is just right on Venus!
On Mercury, some mold that's green and furry!
Blbblblbl
Pshhh
And for the Sun?

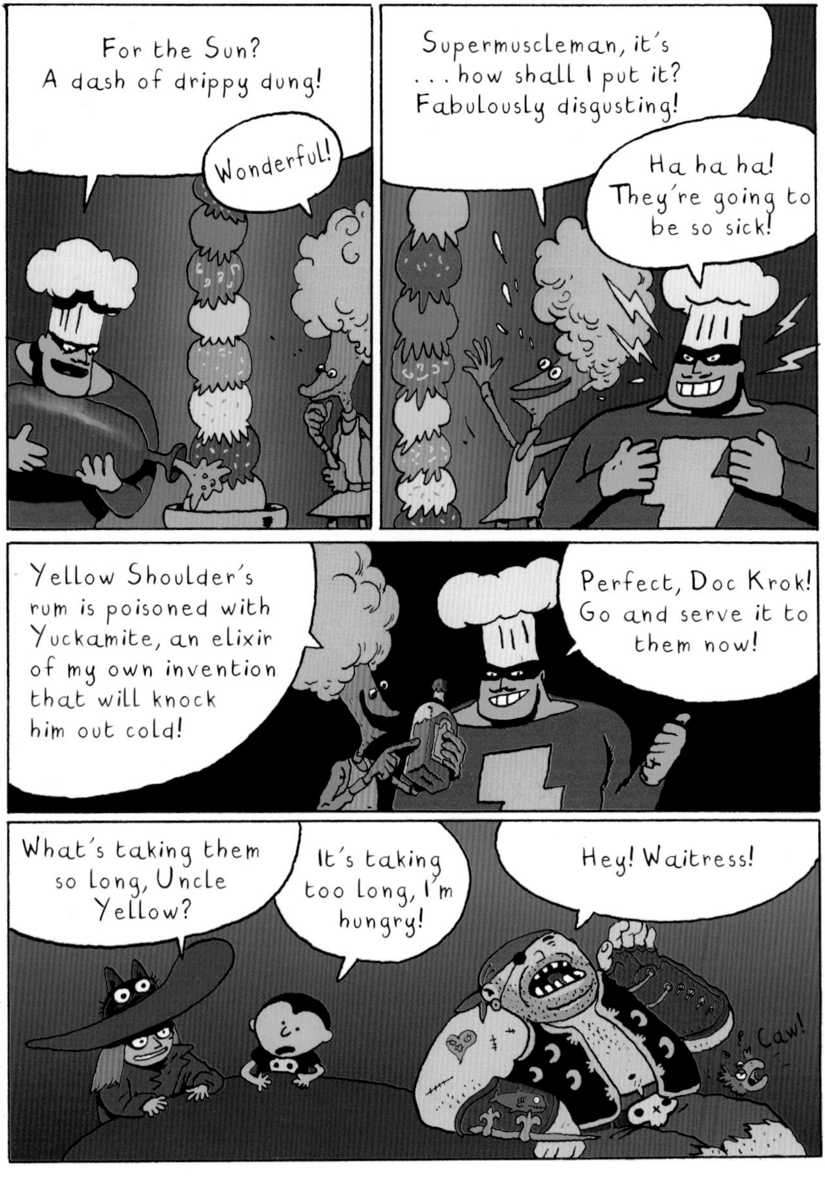
For the Sun? A dash of drippy dung!
Wonderful!
Supermuscleman, it's . . . how shall I put it? Fabulously disgusting!
Ha ha ha! They're going to be so sick!
Yellow Shoulder's rum is poisoned with Yuckamite, an elixir of my own invention that will knock him out cold!
Perfect, Doc Krok! Go and serve it to them now!
What's taking them so long, Uncle Yellow?
It's taking too long, I'm hungry!
Hey! Waitress!
Caw!

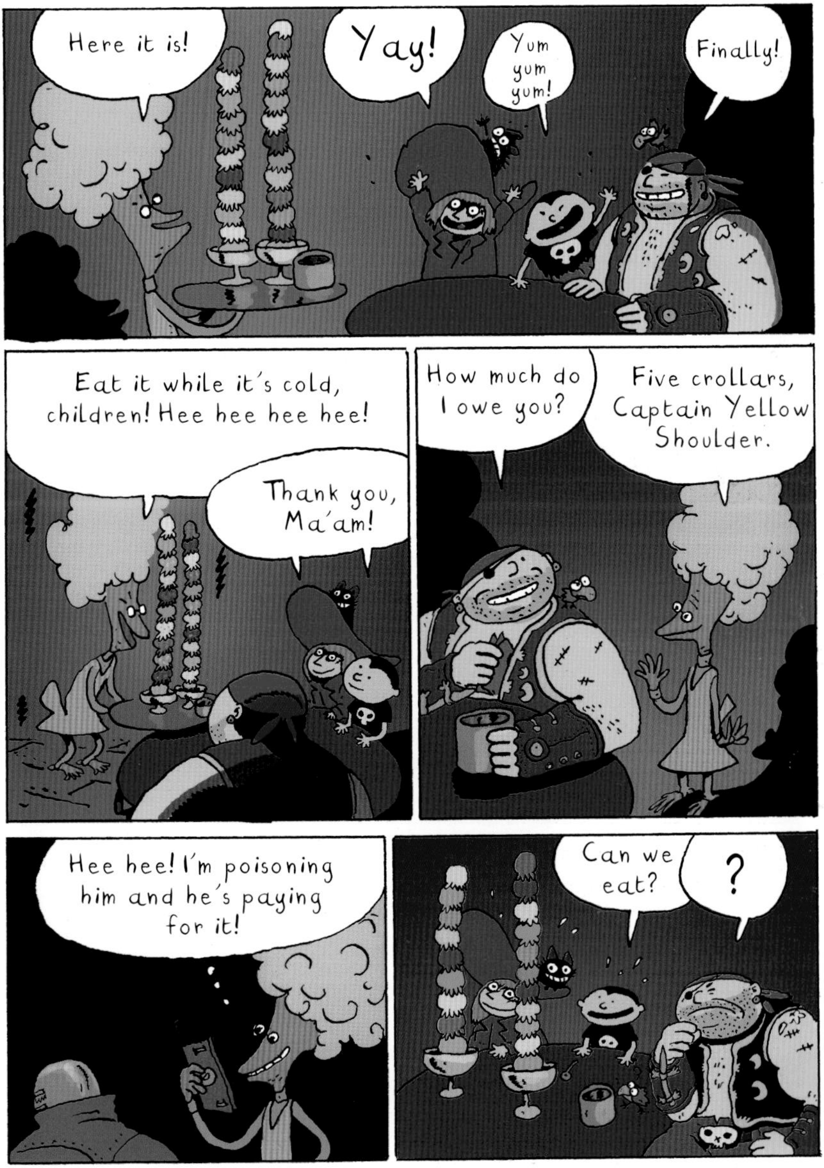
Here it is!
Yay!
Yum yum yum!
Finally!
Eat it while it's cold, children! Hee hee hee hee!
Thank you, Ma'am!
How much do I owe you?
Five crollars, Captain Yellow Shoulder.
Hee hee! I'm poisoning him and he's paying for it!
Can we eat?
?

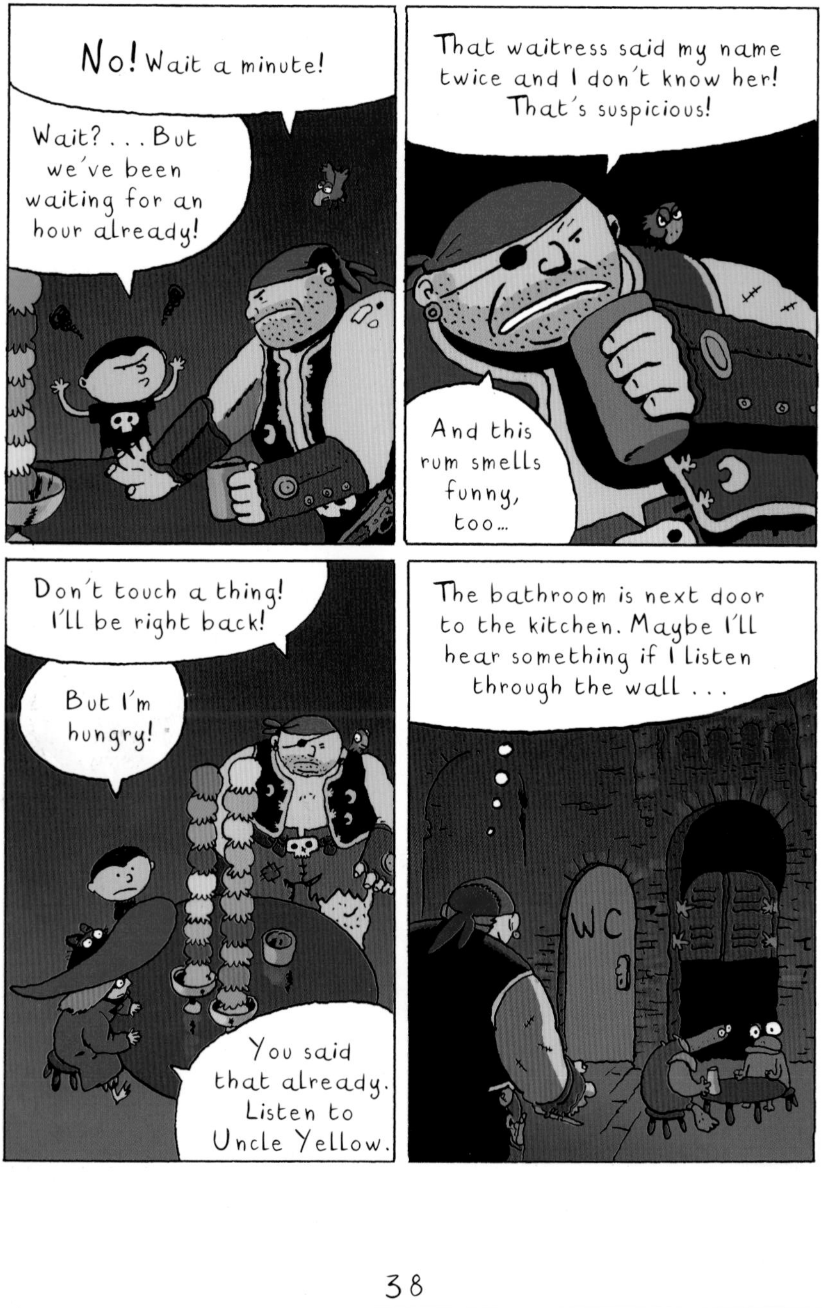
No! Wait a minute!
Wait? . . . But we've been waiting for an hour already!
That waitress said my name twice and I don't know her! That's suspicious!
And this rum smells funny, too...
Don't touch a thing! I'll be right back!
But I'm hungry!
You said that already. Listen to Uncle Yellow.
The bathroom is next door to the kitchen. Maybe I'll hear something if I listen through the wall . . .
WC

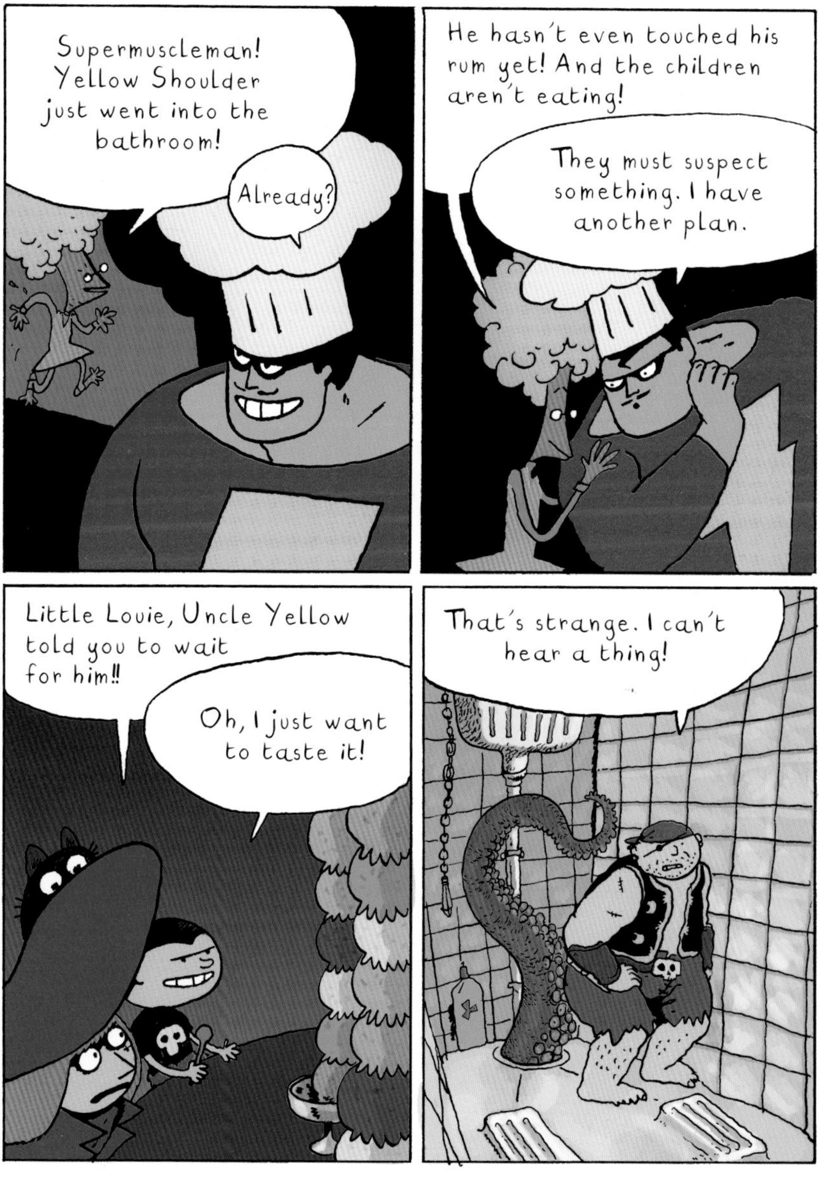
Supermuscleman! Yellow Shoulder just went into the bathroom!
Already?
He hasn't even touched his rum yet! And the children aren't eating!
They must suspect something. I have another plan.
Little Louie, Uncle Yellow told you to wait for him!!
Oh, I just want to taste it!
That's strange. I can't hear a thing!

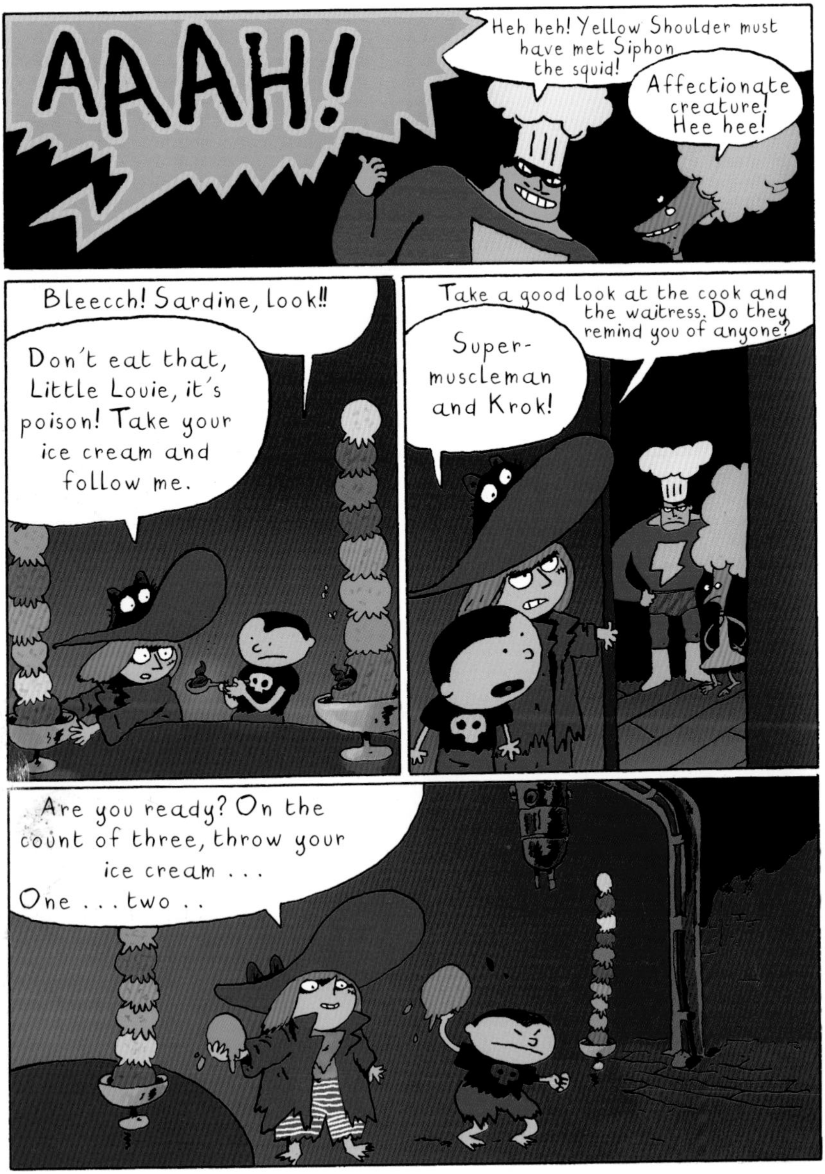
AAAH!
Heh heh! Yellow Shoulder must have met Siphon the squid!
Affectionate creature! Hee hee!
Bleecch! Sardine, look!!
Don't eat that, Little Louie, it's poison! Take your ice cream and follow me.
Take a good look at the cook and the waitress. Do they remind you of anyone?
Super-muscleman and Krok!
Are you ready? On the count of three, throw your ice cream . . .
One . . . two . .

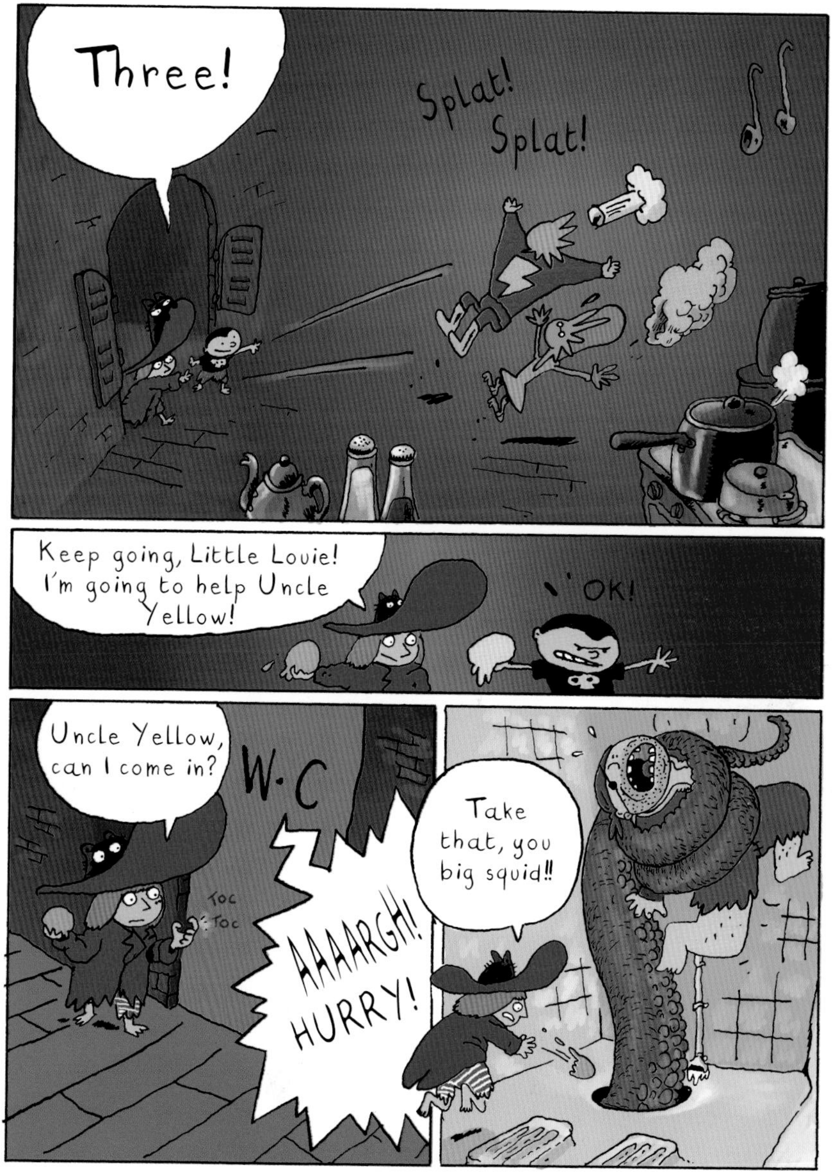
Three!
Splat! Splat!
Keep going, Little Louie! I'm going to help Uncle Yellow!
OK!
Uncle Yellow, can I come in?
W.C
TOC TOC
AAAARGH! HURRY!
Take that, you big squid!!

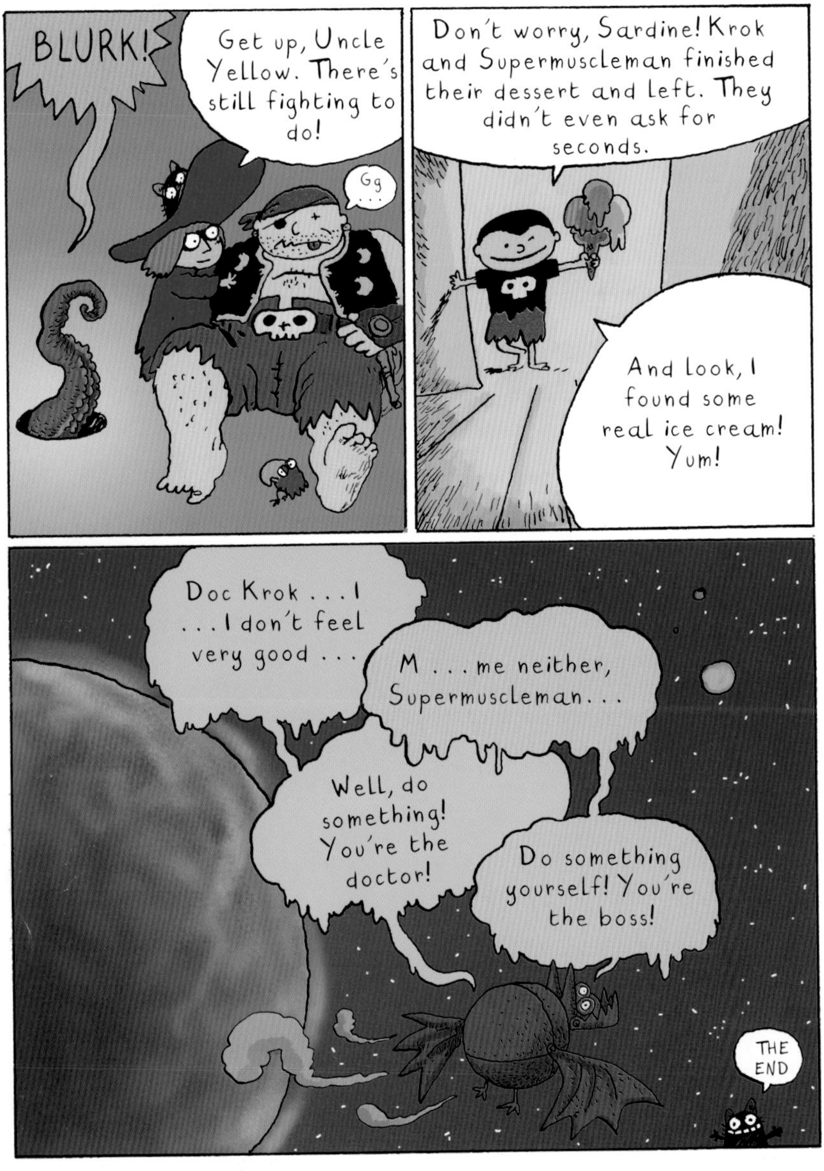
BLURK!
Get up, Uncle Yellow. There's still fighting to do!
Gg . . .
Don't worry, Sardine! Krok and Supermuscleman finished their dessert and left. They didn't even ask for seconds.
And look, I found some real ice cream! Yum!
Doc Krok . . . I . . . I don't feel very good . . .
M . . . me neither, Supermuscleman . . .
Well, do something! You're the doctor!
Do something yourself! You're the boss!
THE END

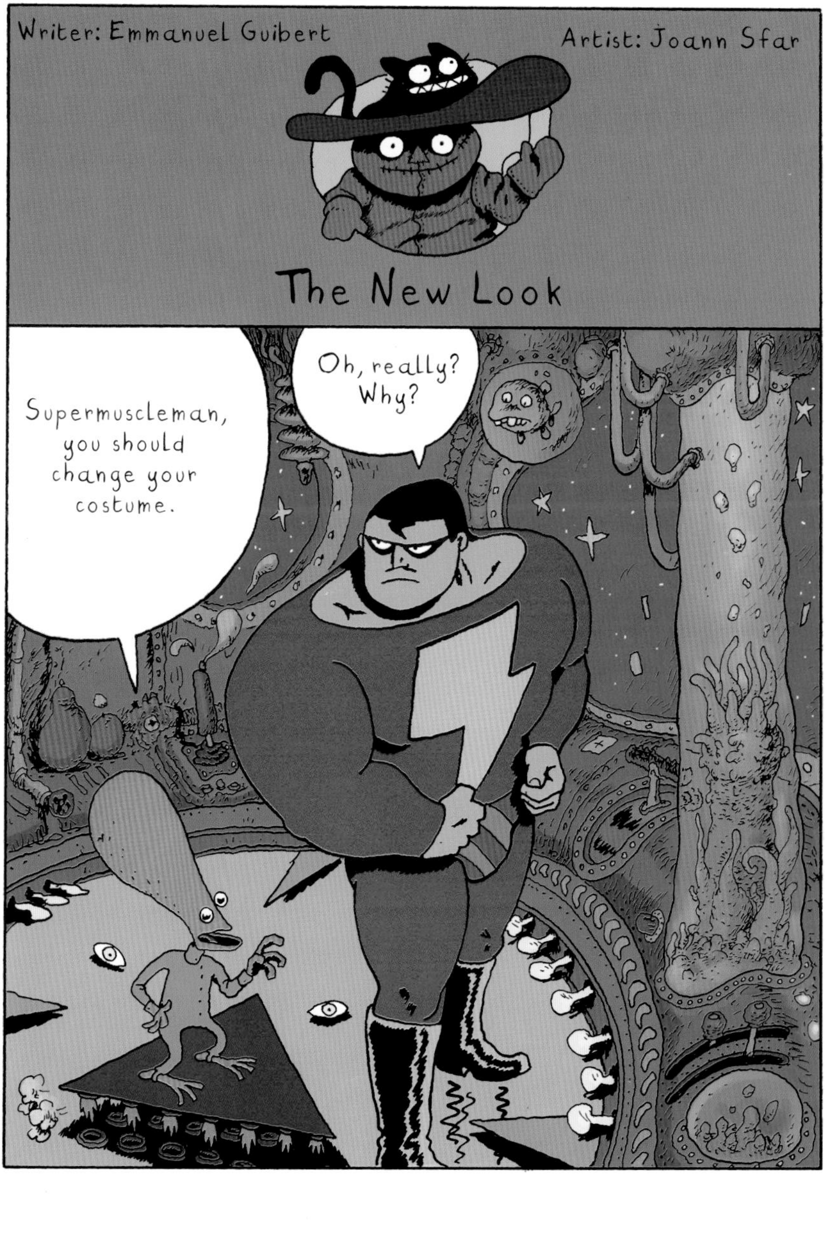
Writer: Emmanuel Guibert
Artist: Joann Sfar
The New Look
Supermuscleman, you should change your costume.
Oh, really? Why?

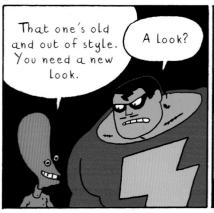

That one's old and out of style. You need a new look.

A look?

Yes, a different appearance. Bad guys are supposed to look nice nowadays.

Are you sure about that, Doc Krok?

Think about it! A bad guy who looks bad sends everyone running. Then there's no one to do bad stuff to . . .

Hmm . . .

Whereas a bad guy who looks nice attracts people to him. Especially children. And once he's got them, he can be really, really bad.

Hee hee . . . Not a bad idea!

We're heading for the planet Overalls. We'll find something for your new look there!

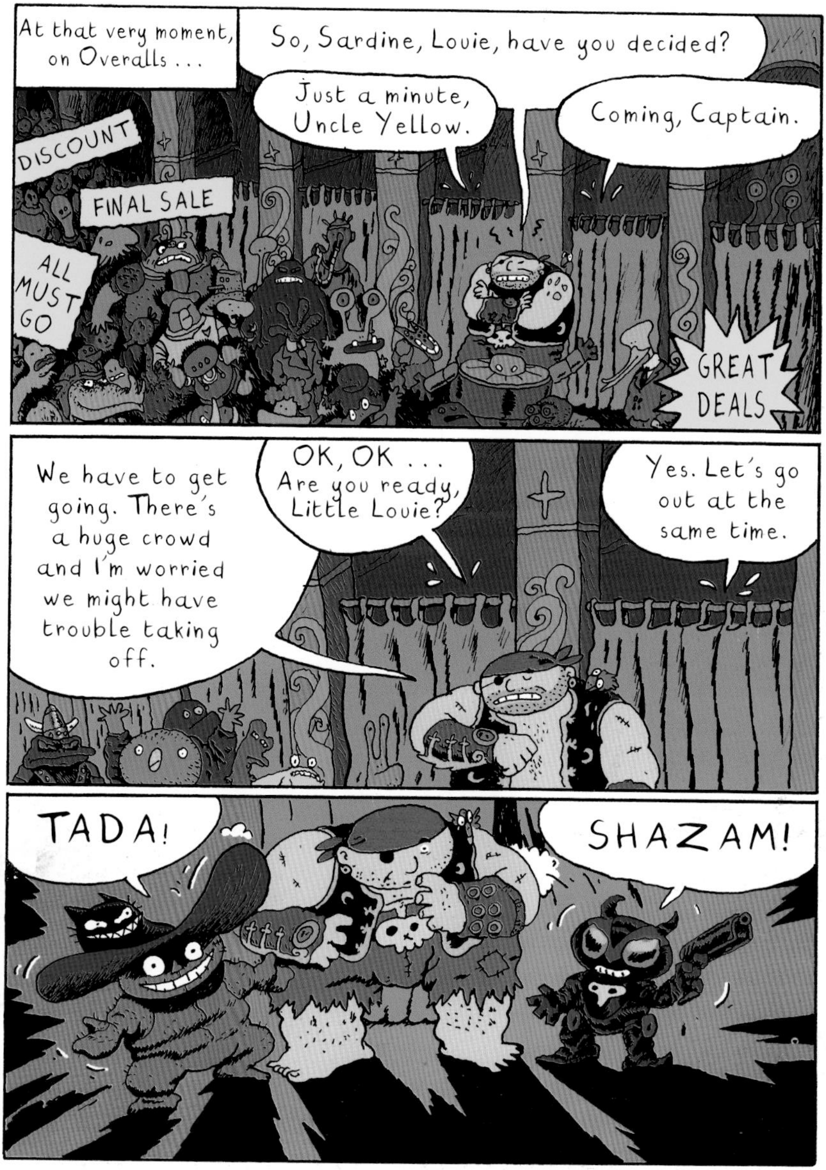
At that very moment, on Overalls . . .
So, Sardine, Louie, have you decided?
Just a minute, Uncle Yellow.
Coming, Captain.
DISCOUNT
FINAL SALE
ALL MUST GO
GREAT DEALS
We have to get going. There's a huge crowd and I'm worried we might have trouble taking off.
OK, OK . . . Are you ready, Little Louie?
Yes. Let's go out at the same time.
TADA!
SHAZAM!

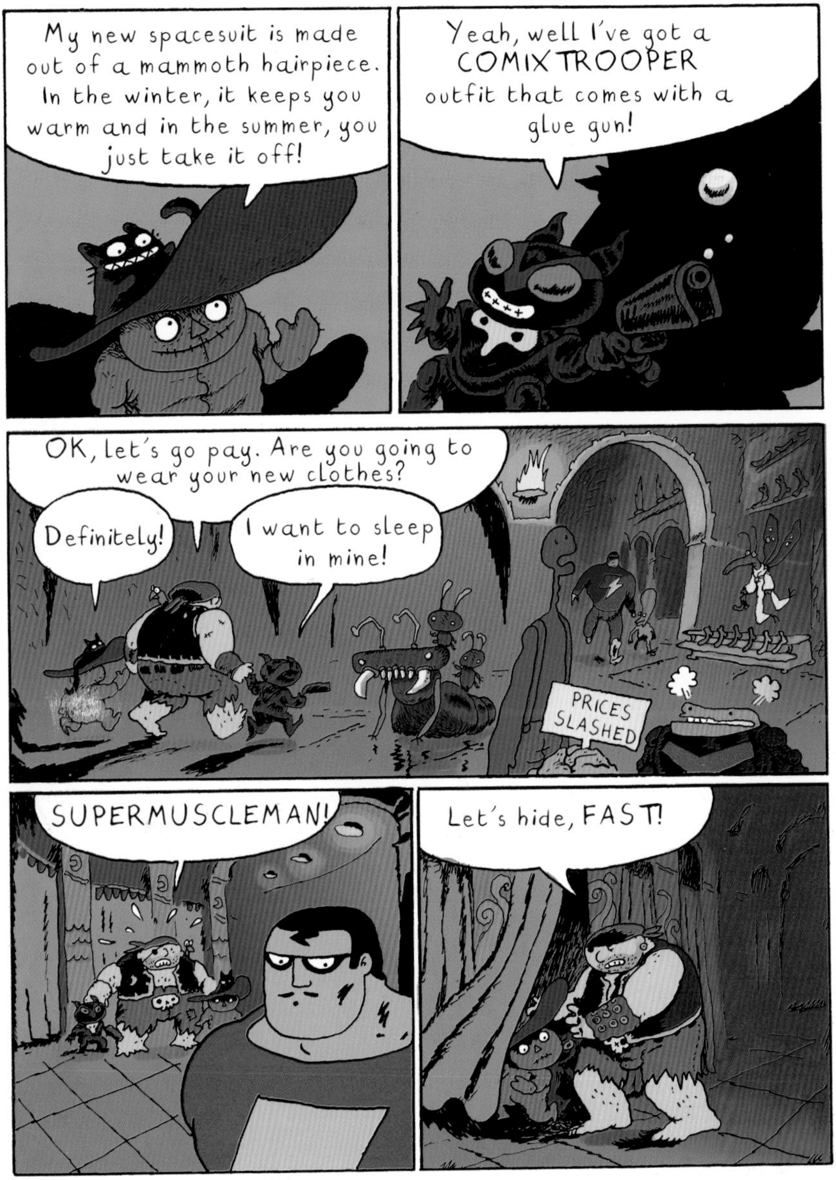
My new spacesuit is made out of a mammoth hairpiece. In the winter, it keeps you warm and in the summer, you just take it off!
Yeah, well I've got a COMIXTROOPER outfit that comes with a glue gun!
OK, let's go pay. Are you going to wear your new clothes?
Definitely!
I want to sleep in mine!
PRICES SLASHED
SUPERMUSCLEMAN!
Let's hide, FAST!

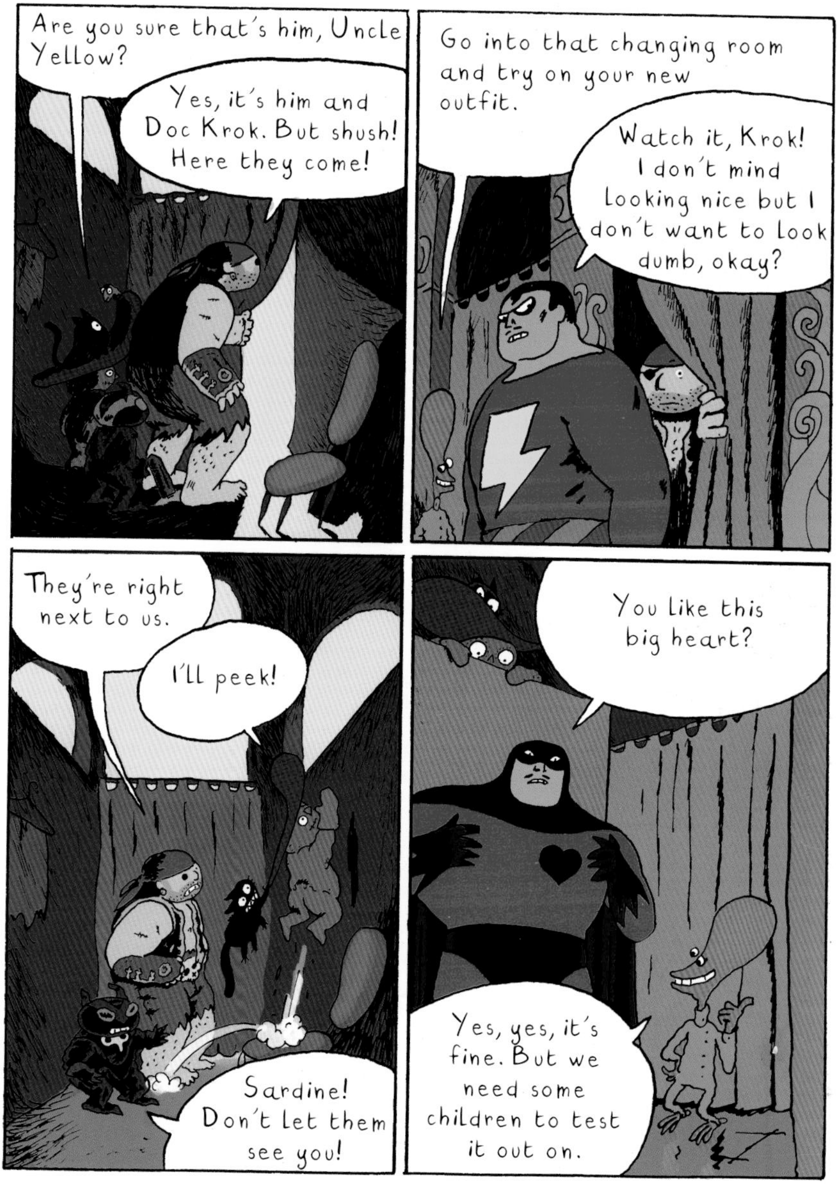
Are you sure that's him, Uncle Yellow?
Yes, it's him and Doc Krok. But shush! Here they come!
Go into that changing room and try on your new outfit.
Watch it, Krok! I don't mind looking nice but I don't want to look dumb, okay?
They're right next to us.
I'll peek!
Sardine! Don't let them see you!
You like this big heart?
Yes, yes, it's fine. But we need some children to test it out on.

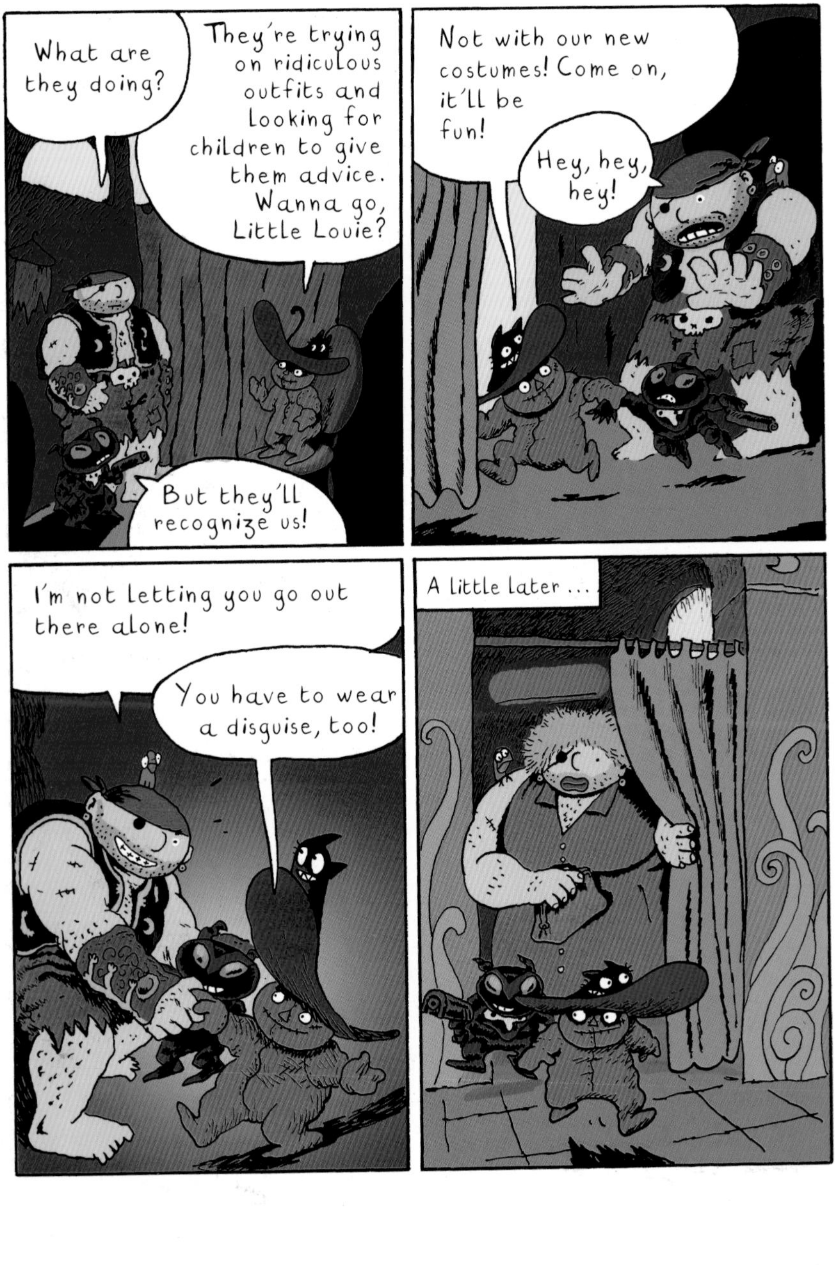
What are they doing?
They're trying on ridiculous outfits and looking for children to give them advice. Wanna go, Little Louie?
But they'll recognize us!
Not with our new costumes! Come on, it'll be fun!
Hey, hey, hey!
I'm not letting you go out there alone!
You have to wear a disguise, too!
A little later ...

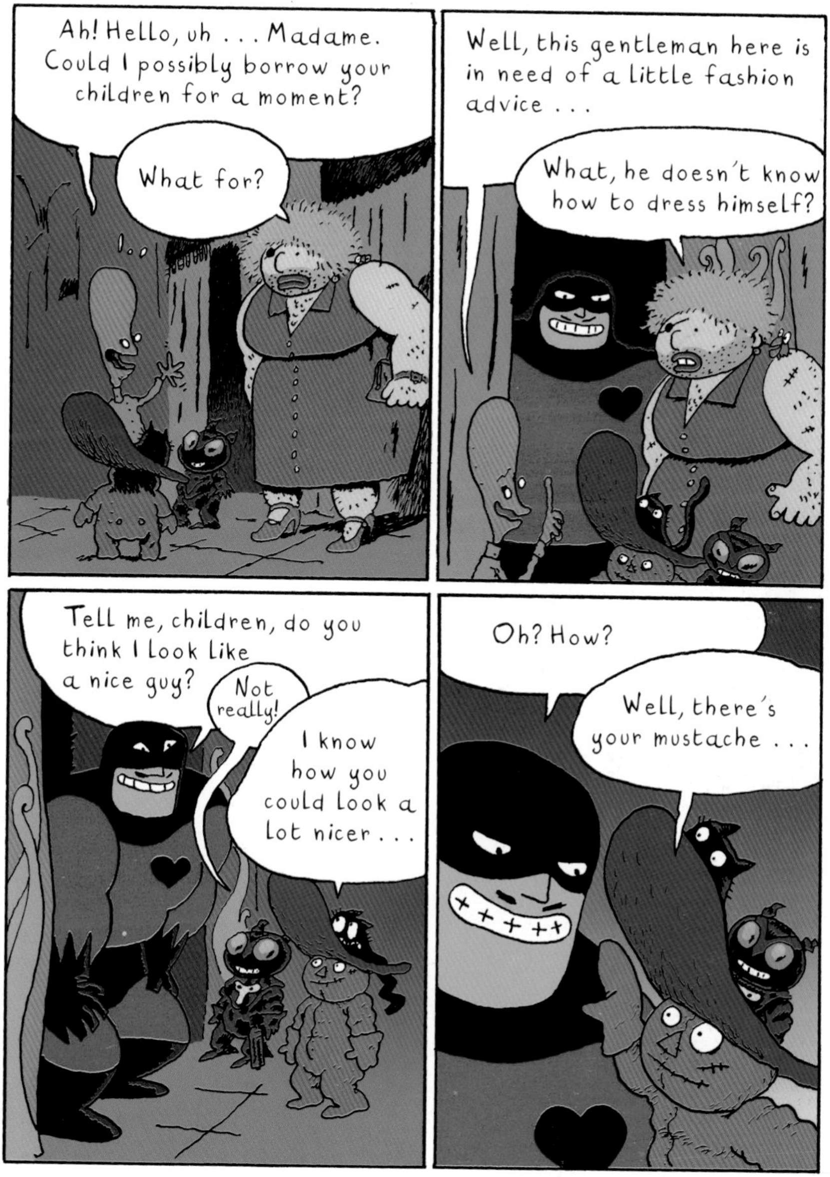
Ah! Hello, uh . . . Madame. Could I possibly borrow your children for a moment?
What for?
Well, this gentleman here is in need of a little fashion advice . . .
What, he doesn't know how to dress himself?
Tell me, children, do you think I look like a nice guy?
Not really!
I know how you could look a lot nicer . . .
Oh? How?
Well, there's your mustache . . .

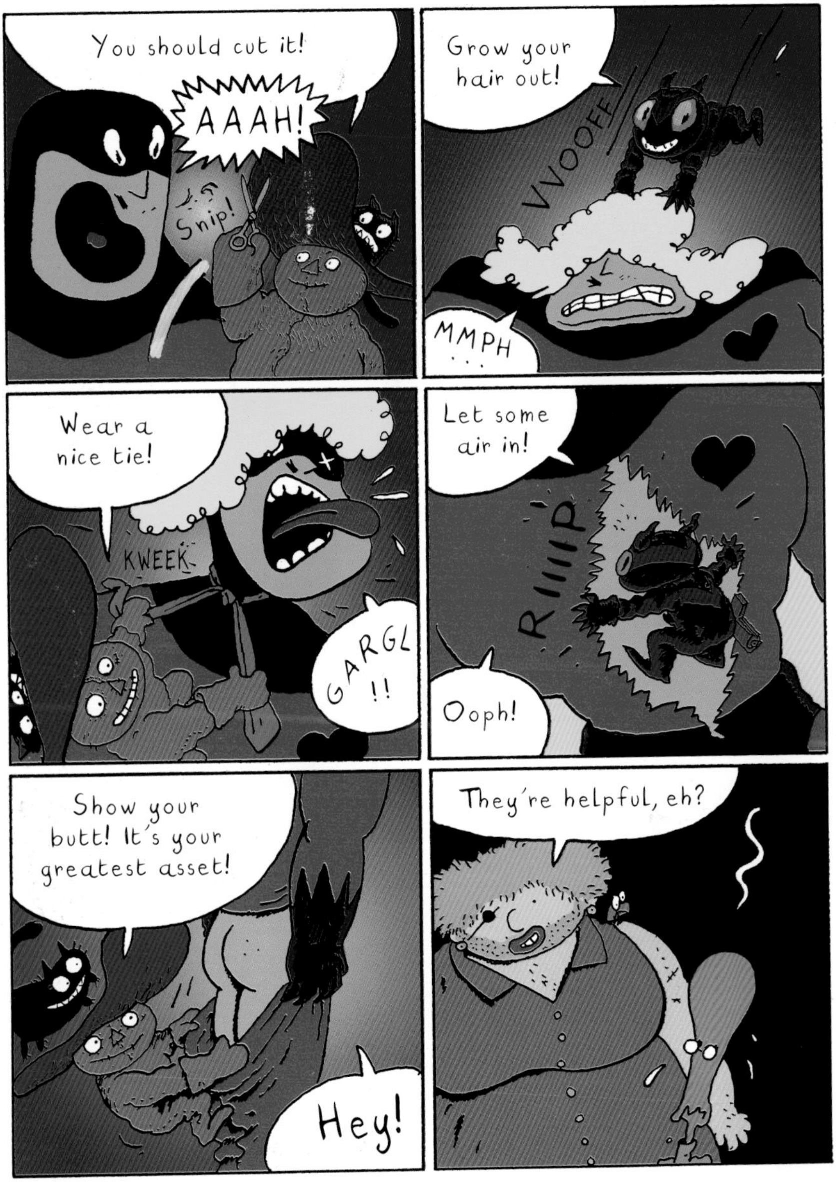
You should cut it!
AAAH!
Snip!
Grow your hair out!
VVOOFF
MMPH...
Wear a nice tie!
KWEEK
GARGL!!
Let some air in!
RIIIIIP
Ooph!
Show your butt! It's your greatest asset!
Hey!
They're helpful, eh?

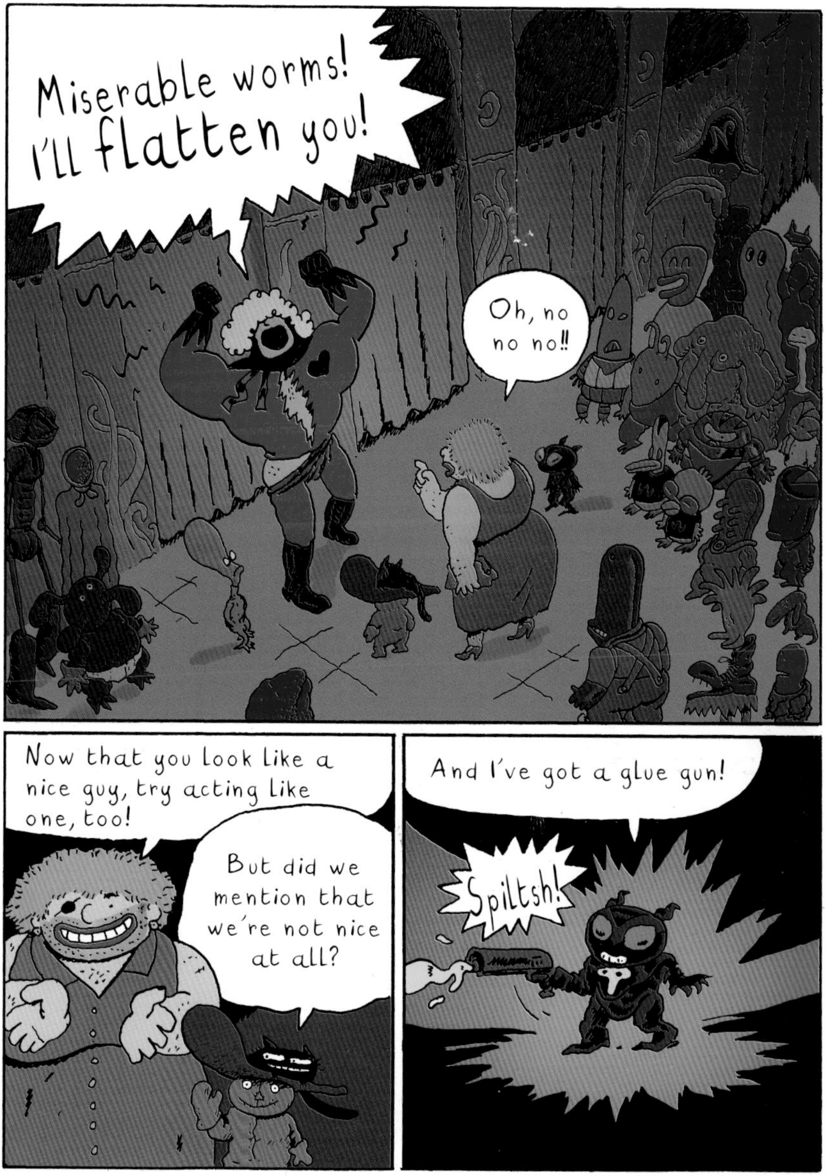
Miserable worms! I'LL flatten you!
Oh, no no no!!
Now that you look like a nice guy, try acting like one, too!
But did we mention that we're not nice at all?
And I've got a glue gun!
Spiltsh!

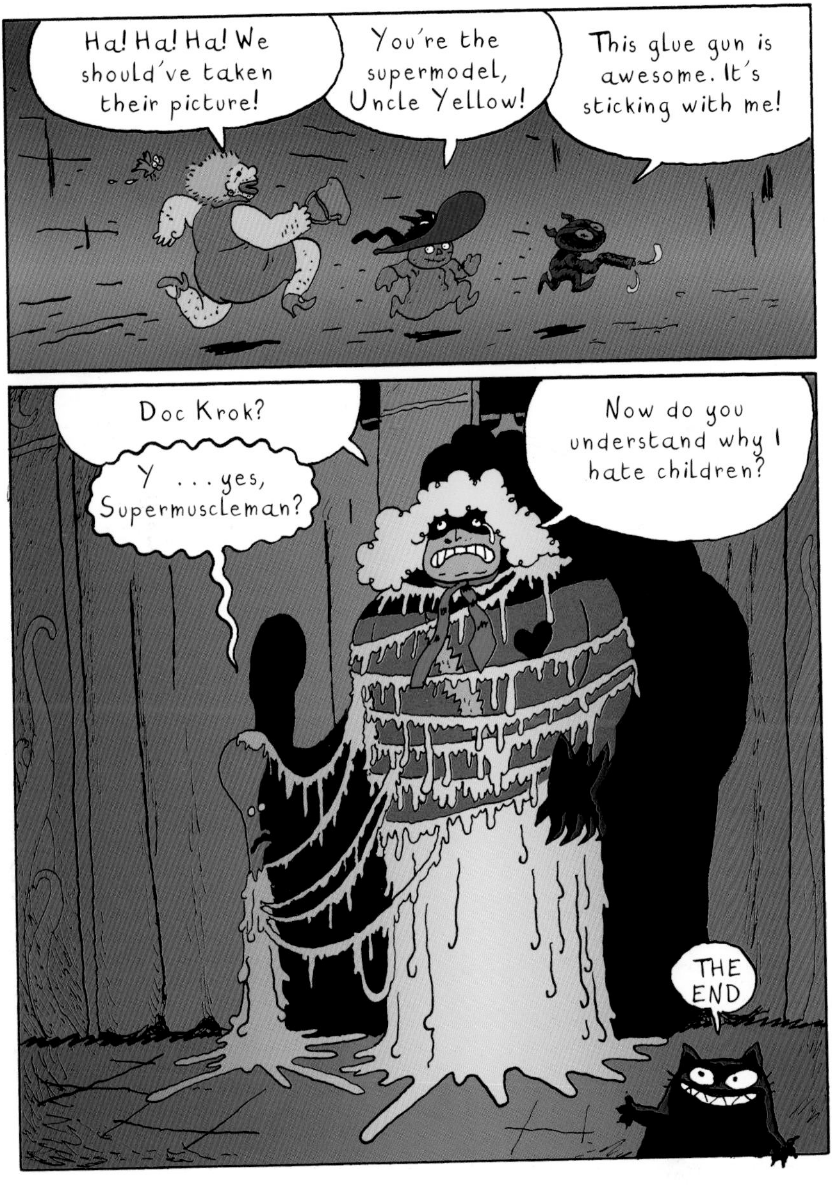
Ha! Ha! Ha! We should've taken their picture!
You're the supermodel, Uncle Yellow!
This glue gun is awesome. It's sticking with me!
Doc Krok?
Y ...yes, Supermuscleman?
Now do you understand why I hate children?
THE END

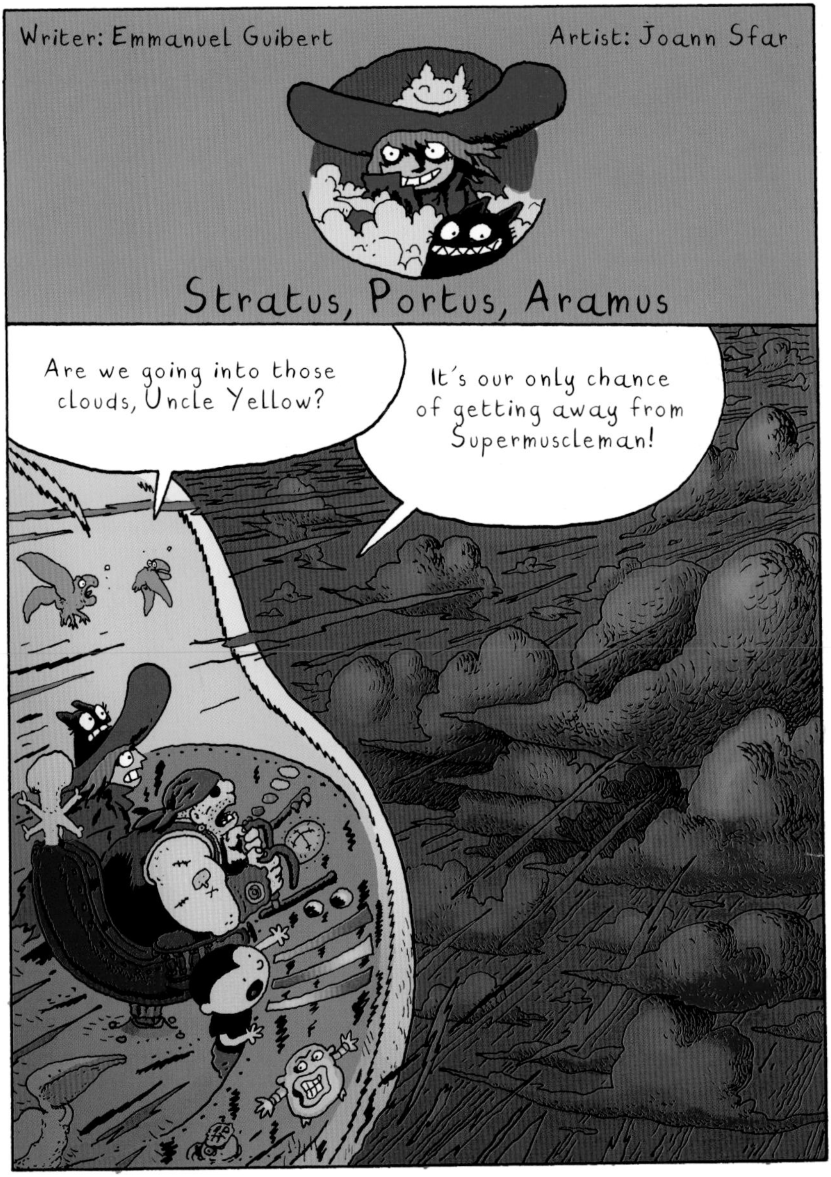
Writer: Emmanuel Guibert
Artist: Joann Sfar
Stratus, Portus, Aramus
Are we going into those clouds, Uncle Yellow?
It's our only chance of getting away from Supermuscleman!

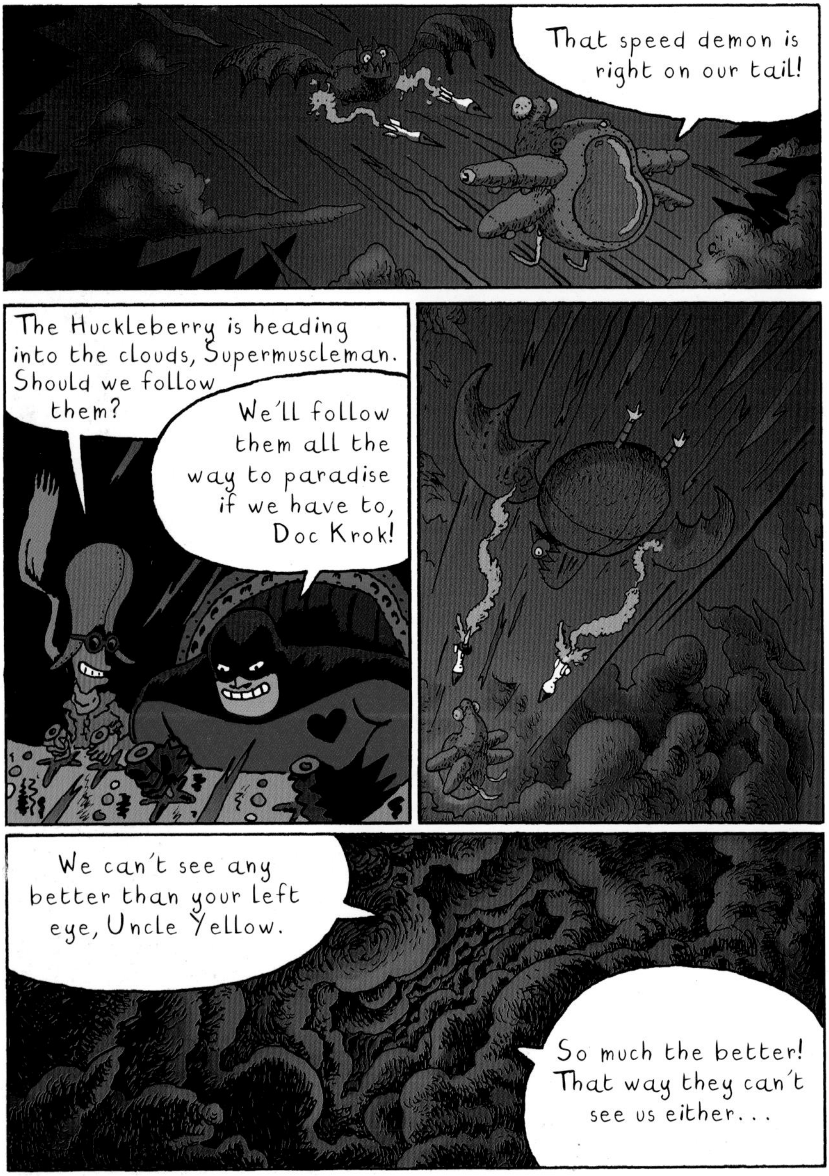
That speed demon is right on our tail!
The Huckleberry is heading into the clouds, Supermuscleman. Should we follow them?
We'll follow them all the way to paradise if we have to, Doc Krok!
We can't see any better than your left eye, Uncle Yellow.
So much the better! That way they can't see us either...

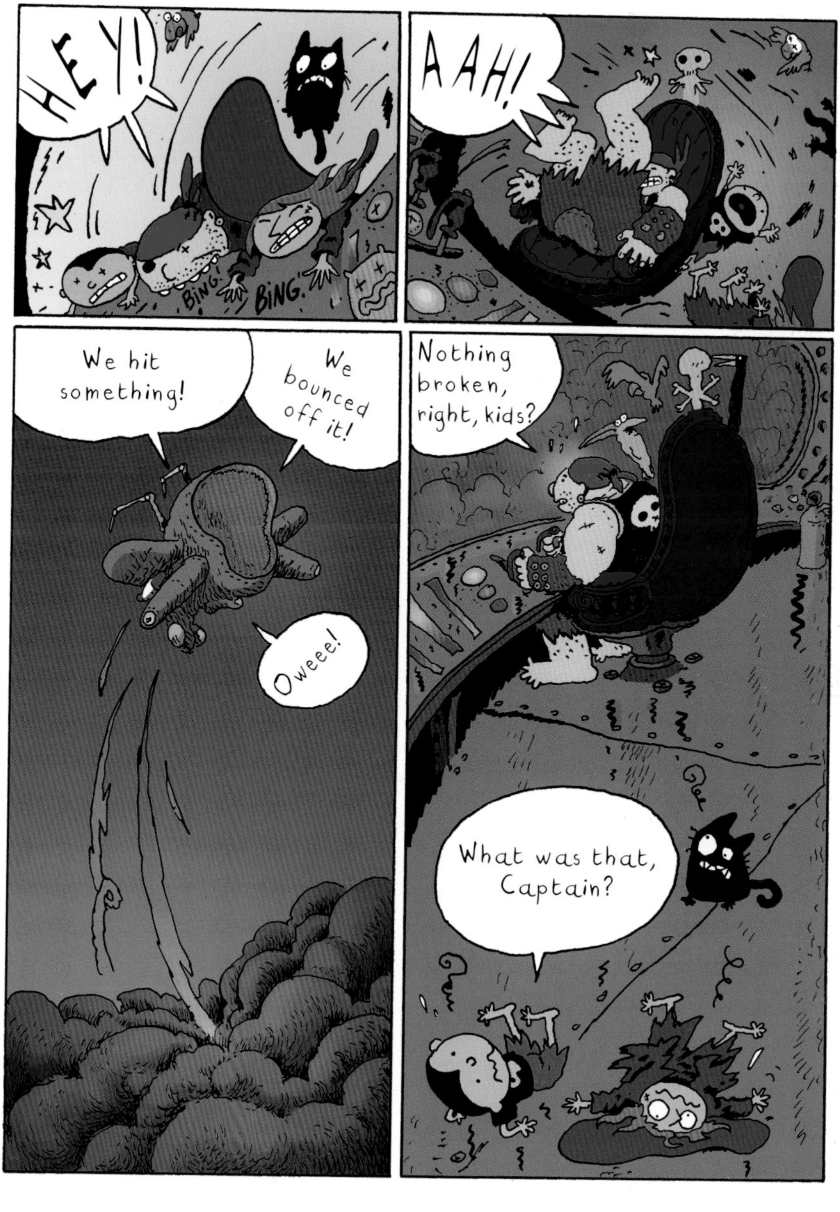
HEY!
BING!
BING!
AAH!
We hit something!
We bounced off it!
Oweee!
Nothing broken, right, kids?
What was that, Captain?

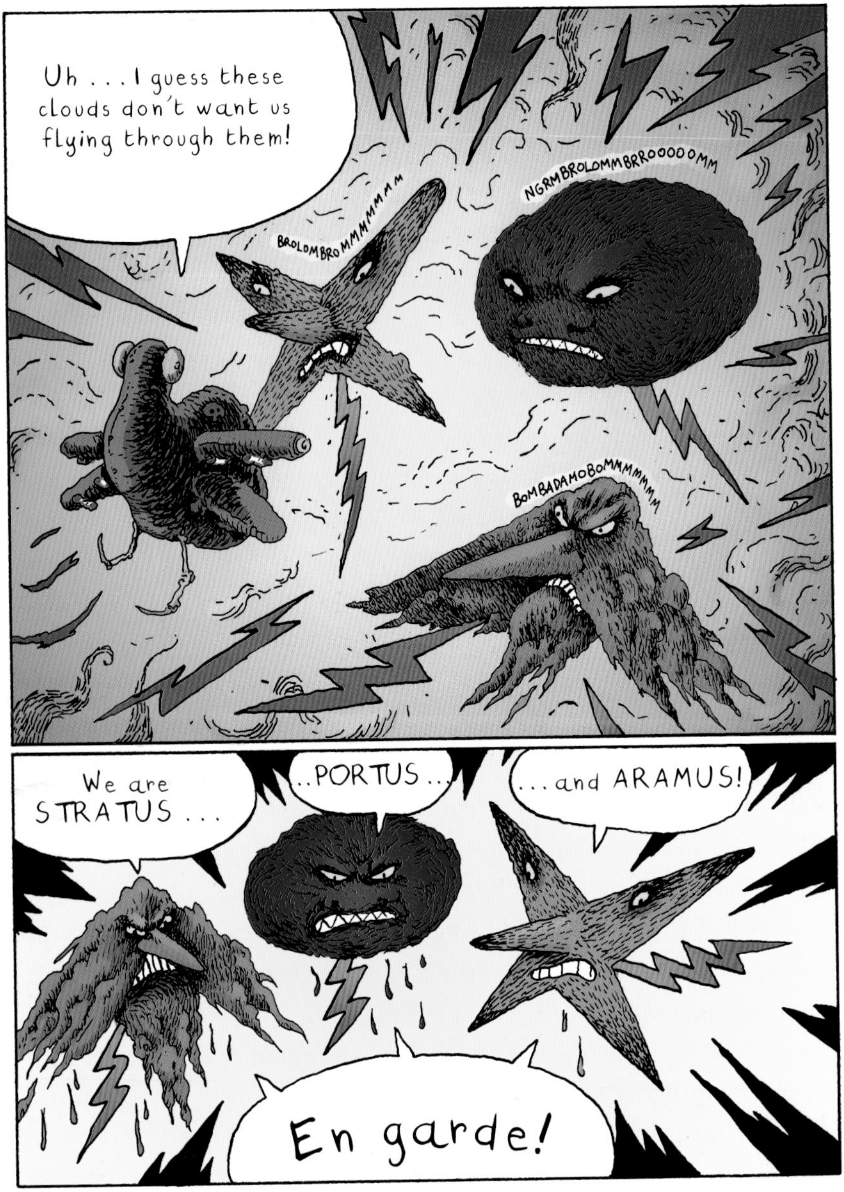
Uh . . . I guess these clouds don't want us flying through them!
BROLOMBROMMMMMMMMM
NGRMBROLOMMBRROOOOOOMM
BOMBADAMOBOMMMMMMM
We are STRATUS . . .
..PORTUS ..
. . . and ARAMUS!
En garde!

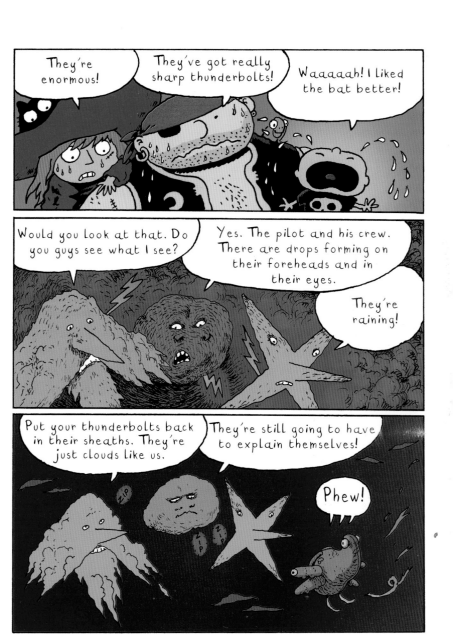

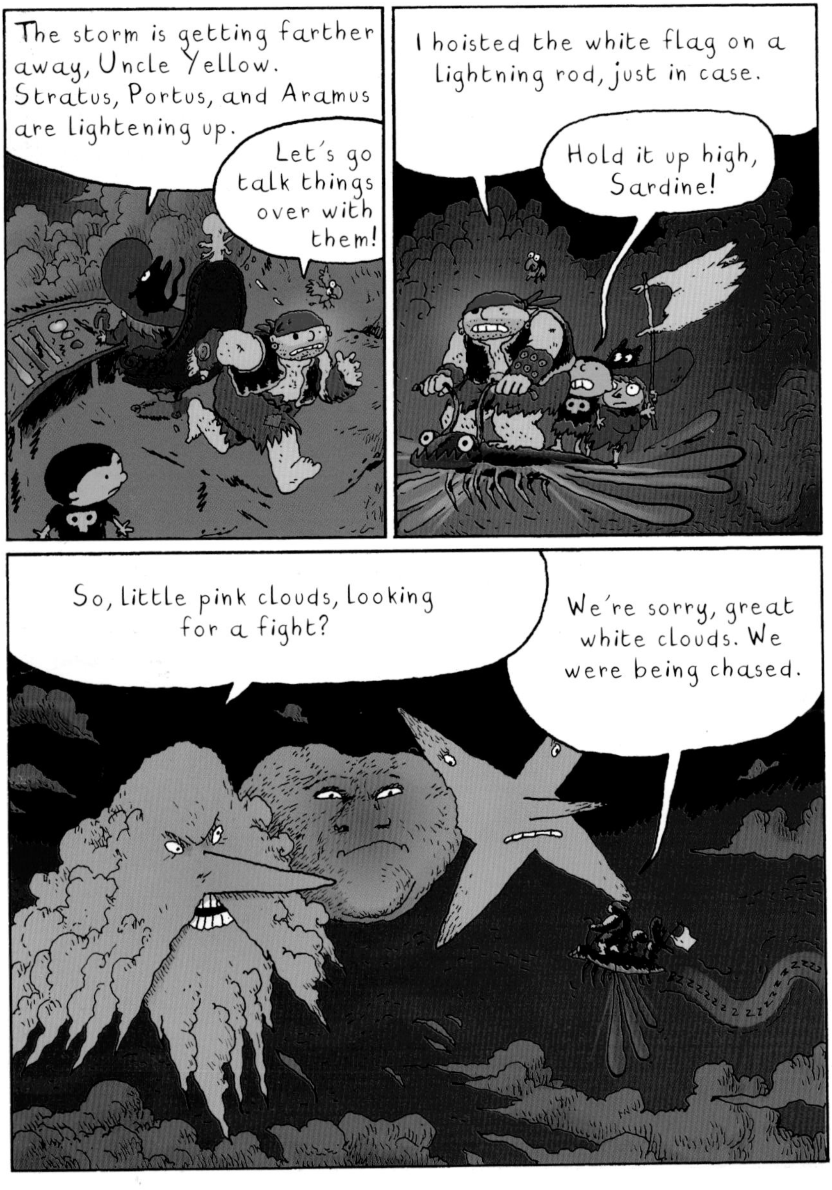
The storm is getting farther away, Uncle Yellow. Stratus, Portus, and Aramus are lightening up.
Let's go talk things over with them!
I hoisted the white flag on a lightning rod, just in case.
Hold it up high, Sardine!
So, little pink clouds, looking for a fight?
We're sorry, great white clouds. We were being chased.

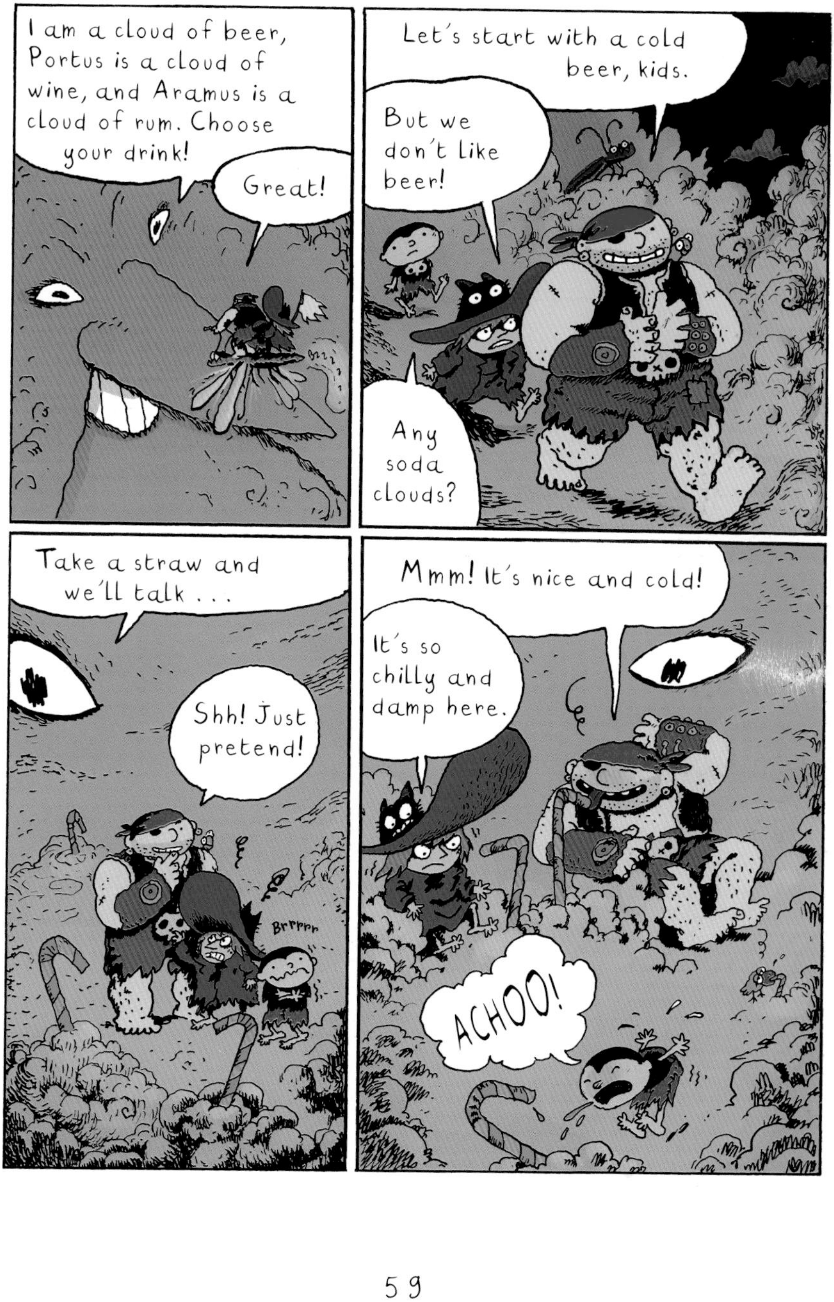
I am a cloud of beer, Portus is a cloud of wine, and Aramus is a cloud of rum. Choose your drink!
Great!
Let's start with a cold beer, kids.
But we don't like beer!
Any soda clouds?
Take a straw and we'll talk . . .
Shh! Just pretend!
Brrrrr
Mmm! It's nice and cold!
It's so chilly and damp here.
ACHOO!

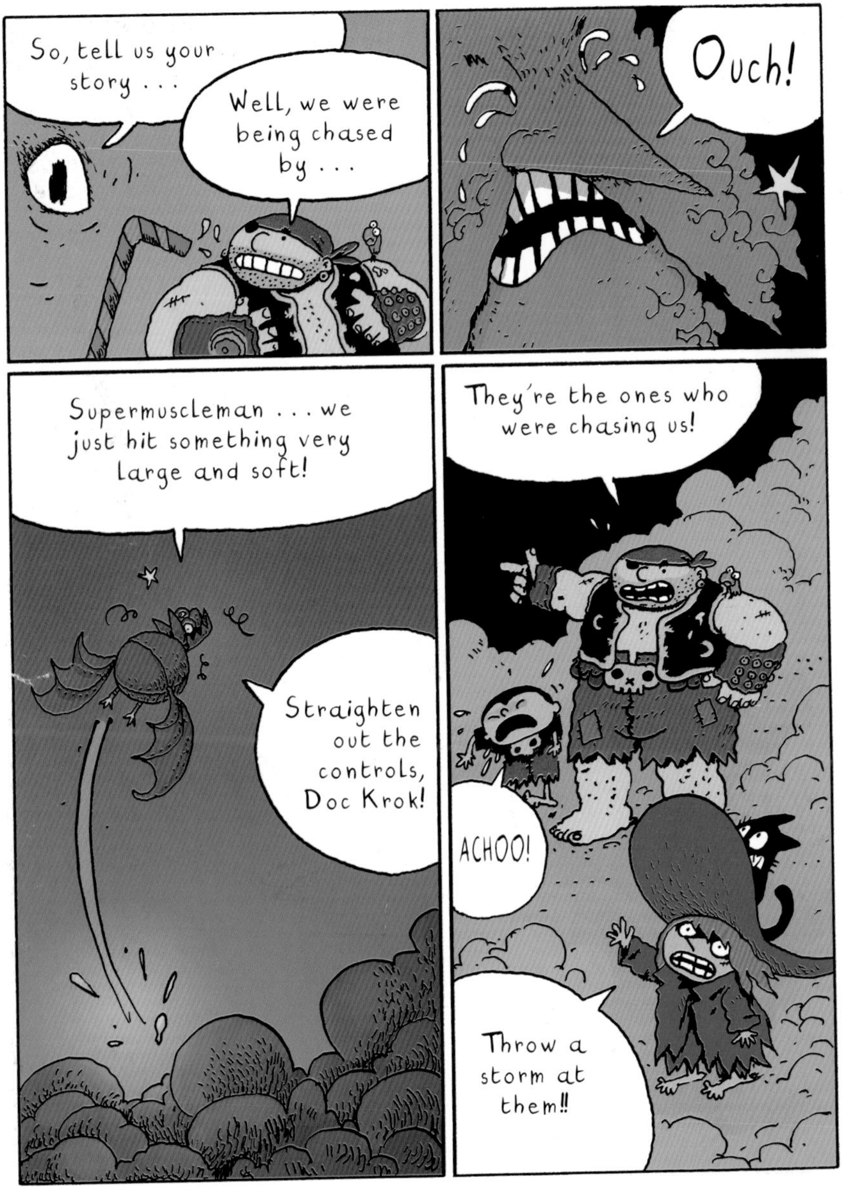
So, tell us your story . . .
Well, we were being chased by . . .
Ouch!
Supermuscleman . . . we just hit something very large and soft!
Straighten out the controls, Doc Krok!
They're the ones who were chasing us!
ACHOO!
Throw a storm at them!!

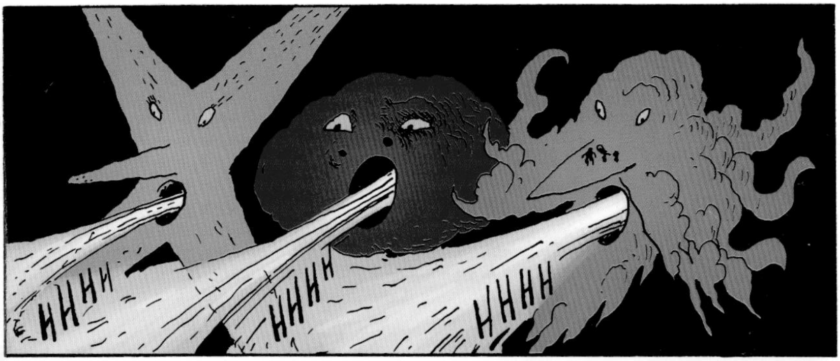
HHHH
HHHH
HHHH

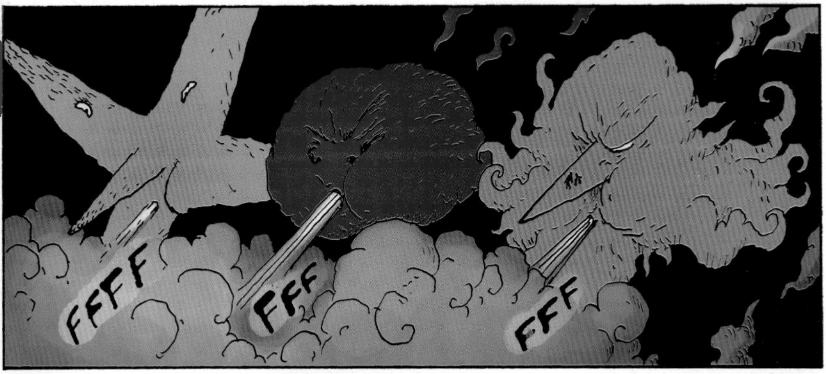
FFFF
FFF
FFF

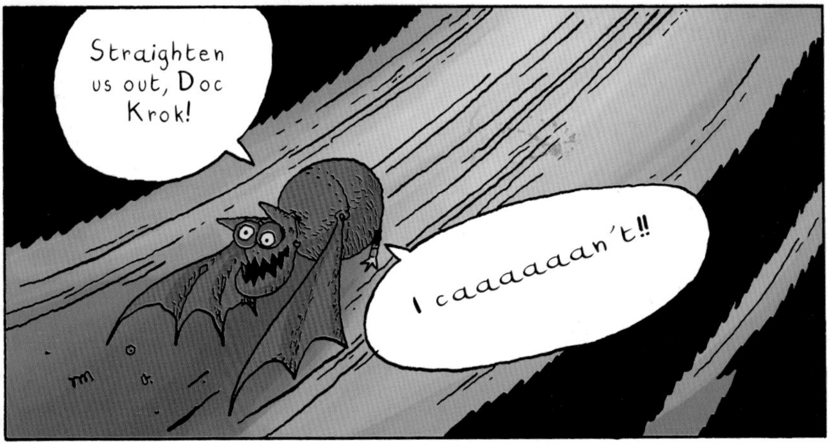
Straighten us out, Doc Krok!
I caaaaaaan't!!

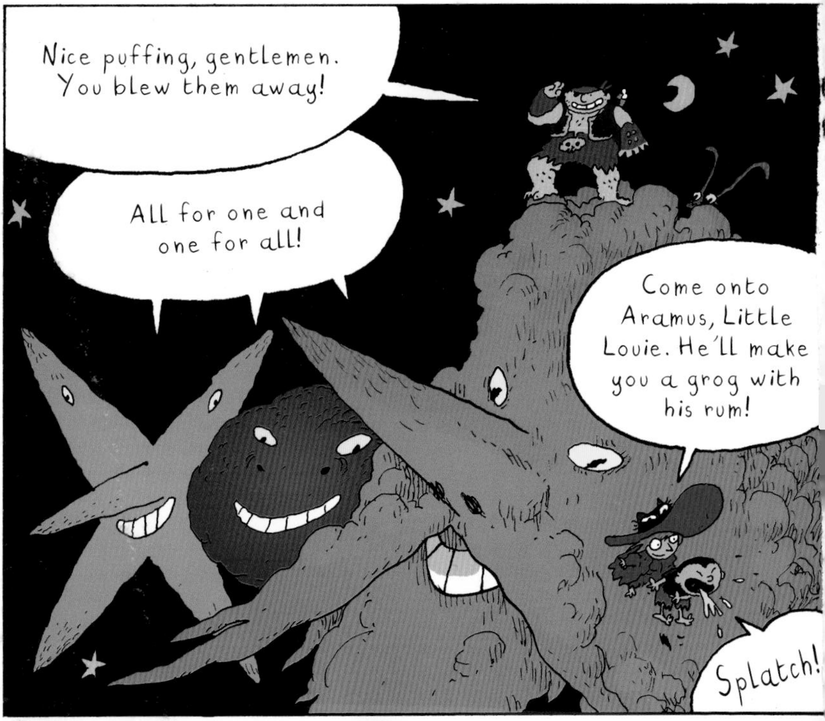
Nice puffing, gentlemen. You blew them away!
All for one and one for all!
Come onto Aramus, Little Louie. He'll make you a grog with his rum!
Splatch!

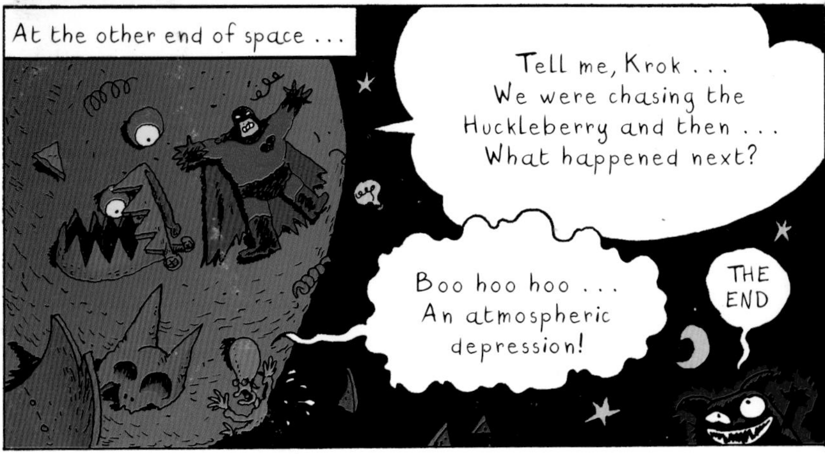
At the other end of space . . .
Tell me, Krok . . . We were chasing the Huckleberry and then . . . What happened next?
Boo hoo hoo . . . An atmospheric depression!
THE END